Don't Trust Beth Harper

Andboo

Beth Harper arrives at Oakridge High as a mystery—and within days, everyone knows her name.

Effortlessly charming jocks and queen bees comes easy for her,

but Beth doesn't care to fit in,

she thrives on chaos.

But Oakridge runs on whispers,

and as rumors collide with secrets,

the cracks begin to show.

As dangerous truths from Beth's past
threaten to surface,

she'll do whatever it takes to keep them
buried.

Beth Harper

senior - new girl

Samantha Rivera
junior - cheer captain

Jenna Thomas
senior - co-captain

Alex Harding
senior - quarterback

Jake Jacobs
senior - running back

Patty Patrick
senior - queen bee

Mia Marlow
junior - class president

Your Name
?? - book club

Mike Halk
senior - tennis

Lainey Smith
junior - yearbook

Ryan Andrews
sophomore - journalism

Benny Smith
freshman - basketball

Brian James
freshman - football

Riley Ross
senior - cheerleader

Sarah Fitz
sophomore - cheerleader

Kayla Taylor
junior - cheerleader

Debra Dobbs
sophomore - spirit squad

Official Teaser Trailer

(Available On Most Social Platforms)

https://sites.google.com/view/andboo/dtbh-trailers

Official Music Playlist

(Available On Most Social Platforms)

https://sites.google.com/view/endboo/book-playlists/dtbh-playlists

Chapter 1: Homecoming - 1

Chapter 2: Beth's Entrance - 9

Chapter 3: Homeroom - 13

Chapter 4: An Intriguing Invitation - 20

Chapter 5: Football Practice - 28

Chapter 6: Patty's Pool Party - 33

Chapter 7: Not So Cinderella - 43

Chapter 8: Not So Sleeping Beauty - 49

Chapter 9: Wake Up, Whore - 58

Chapter 10: Manic Monday - 65

Chapter 11: The Rumors Are True - 74

Chapter 12: Dramaleaders - 80

Chapter 13: More Enemies Than Friends - 85

Chapter 14: The Social Pyramid - 91

Chapter 15: A Strange Alliance - 98

Chapter 16: The Day I Met The Devil - 104

Chapter 17: Saturday Night Haze - 111

Chapter 18: Girls Like Trouble - 125

Chapter 19: I Kissed a Girl - 132

Chapter 20: Same Sam - 146

Chapter 21: Jail Bait - 152

Chapter 22: Hoe Hoe Hotel - 162

Chapter 23: You, Me, and Marriott - 167

Chapter 24: Beth's New Toy - 172

Chapter 25: Let It Reign - 180

Chapter 26: On a Tuesday? - 188

Chapter 27: Splitting Hairs - 195

Chapter 28: Locker Room Lovers - 203

Chapter 29: A Familiar Face - 210

Chapter 30: Beth's Ex - 218

Chapter 31: Maybe It Gets Better: 227

Chapter 32: Snake & Apple - 233

Chapter 33: Boiled Frog - 238

Chapter 34: A Change of Heart - 250

Chapter 35: Spring Break Madness - 257

Chapter 36: Oops... - 267

Chapter 37: Prom Night - 274

Chapter 38: Digging Up Her Past - 282

Chapter 39: Pretty Little Liar - 287

Chapter 40: Graduation Shenanigans - 291

Chapter 41: Jailhouse Daughter - 300

Chapter 42: Buried in Dirt - 305

Chapter 43: Unanswered Questions - 313

Chapter 44: I've Got the Proof - 322

Chapter 45: The Setup - 328

Chapter 46: It's All Over, Love - 336

Chapter 1
Homecoming

Against the early-September dark, the stadium lights burned white-hot, transforming the field into a bright green island amidst a sea of red-and-gold school colors. The home side bleachers were packed with parents in team hoodies, little kids waving foam fingers, and cheerleaders glittering under the lights like living sequins. The visitor side was half-empty and quiet. Everyone knew Oakridge was going to win this one.

Beth stood alone near the chain-link fence behind the end zone, thirty yards from the nearest cluster of students. Hood up, hands shoved deep in the front pocket of an oversized sweatshirt she'd stolen from her ex. The sleeves swallowed her hands. She didn't want anyone to notice her yet. Not tonight.

She wasn't here to cheer.

She was here to watch.

The announcer's voice crackled again—third quarter, 28–7 Oakridge— and the crowd erupted as number 23 took the handoff, cut left, then exploded through a gap in the line like the defense had simply decided not to exist... but Beth's eyes were on the quarterback. He moved different than the other boys. Quick, decisive, like he already knew where every gap, every angle, every open blade of grass would be before the play even started. He threw his fist in the air as his teammate crossed the goal line untouched.

Beth's teeth caught her bottom lip hard enough to sting.

She watched the way the cheer squad rushed the sideline—ponytails whipping, hands clapping, sharp rhythms—and how he barely glanced at them. He found his offensive line instead, slapped helmets, and said something that made the big right tackle laugh so hard he doubled over. Then he looked up toward the stands, scanning, not posing. Just checking.

For a moment, his gaze flickered across hers

A powerful pulse beat in her throat.

She didn't move. Didn't wave. Didn't smile. Just held still and let the dark hoodie and the distance do their job.

♥

The band struck up the fight song. The kickoff sailed high. Alex was already buckling his chinstrap and talking low to the coach on the sideline. Even from here, she could see the ease and confidence in his shoulders, the way he listened with his whole body, head tilted, then nodded once—like whatever was said had already become part of the next play.

She exhaled slowly through her nose.

Tomorrow was her first official day at Oakridge.

New city. New house. New rules. New every-thing.

She didn't do well with new.

But she did her reconnaissance.

And soon she'd make her entrance, but right now, the most important thing in her new life was figuring out who actually ran this place. Not the principal. Not the teachers. The people who mattered when the adults weren't looking.

And number 13—Alex, the quarterback—was clearly one of them.

As the first half ended, the stadium hummed with a low-frequency energy that seemed to vibrate in Beth's chest. The announcer's voice crackled over the speakers, shifting the atmosphere from sport to spectacle.

"Ladies and gentlemen, please direct your attention to the fifty-yard line for the crowning of our Homecoming Royalty!"

She watched as Alex took his helmet off on the sidelines, revealing his divinely chiseled jaw and exquisitely carved sunken eyes.

'He looks like a senior, too,' she thought, *'maybe even older.'*

♥

As the band struck a regal chord, Alex began his stroll toward the makeshift podium. He didn't just walk; he moved with a grounded, effortless confidence that made the frantic energy of the event seem to settle around him. On his way up, the harsh stadium glare caught the sweat on his brow, making him look less like a high school athlete and more like a statue brought to life. Beside him, Patricia Patrick—already draped in a silk sash that looked far too expensive for a football field—beamed at the cameras. She was the perfect counterpart: polished, radiant, and utterly untouchable. Alex didn't seem to care much for Patty; in fact, Beth noticed a subtle, spiteful glare in the way he looked at her.

'An ex?' she thought, a sinister smile crept up her face, *'perfect.'*

There was a gravity in his expression that didn't match the teenage hoopla surrounding them. When the plastic crown was placed on his head, he gave a modest, crooked smile that seemed to pull the air right out of Beth's lungs. For a fleeting second, Patricia leaned in and kissed his cheek, a choreographed moment of perfection that the crowd met with a mixture of deafening ecstatic noises.

The royalty took their lap, the court followed, and the spectacle faded into the frantic warmth of the halftime break. But the grace period was short-lived. The whistle blew, the pageantry was swept away, and the grit of the game returned.

The second half started with Oakridge up big. The game surged forward as they maintained a dominant lead. On the sidelines, the cheerleaders launched into a blur of synchronized leaps and practiced screams, while the brass section of the band blared a triumphant anthem. The student section roared with the restless energy of an impending victory, their voices rising more and more as the minutes bled off the clock, each play moving faster than the last.

♥

Through the chaos, Beth remained silent. She didn't join the chants or the rhythmic clapping; she simply watched the way he moved through the noise.

She glanced up at the scoreboard, startled to find the game had nearly vanished while she was caught in his orbit. The final seconds ticked away. With one final knee to the turf, the stadium erupted in cheer as the clock ran out. Alex didn't pump his chest, he didn't point to the sky, he just pulled his helmet off, shook the sweat out of his hair, and gave the smallest nod toward the student section.

Her lip curled into something that wasn't quite a smile.

She liked that. She liked it a lot.

The crowd flooded the field, but Alex stayed on the sidelines, talking to coaches and fist-bumping teammates. Only when the last of the crowd started drifting toward the parking lot did he finally head for the tunnel.

Beth waited until everyone was almost gone—until the last of the school had disappeared— then she pushed off the fence and started walking home, her heart still hammering, not from nerves, but from hunger. Tomorrow wasn't going to be a fresh start; it was going to be the first day of her hunt.

Chapter 2

Beth's Entrance

The sun hung low in the sky as Beth approached Oakridge High with a mix of excitement and anxiety. Her heart pounded as she wondered how she would be perceived by the students. With her backpack slung over one shoulder, she walked through the imposing iron gates, determined to make her mark.

Once inside the bustling courtyard, she took in the lively scene: students chattering in groups, rushing to classes, and sharing laughter. A deep breath steadied her nerves as she tightened her grip on her bag. With the morning bell echoing through the air, Beth squared her shoulders and began to navigate through the clusters of students. Their curious stares felt like a spotlight shining down on her.

Just as she reached the entrance to the main building, Beth spotted a lanky boy walking toward her, his arms full of books and papers. A mischievous idea struck her. *'Oh, this should add some flair to my entrance,'* she thought. She deliberately stepped into his path, colliding with him and sending his papers scattering across the concrete.

"Watch it!" he exclaimed, kneeling down in a flurry of confusion, trying to gather the fallen papers.

"Move it, nerd," she snapped dismissively, her eyes fixed on a boy in the distance. She continued walking, leaving him bewildered behind her.

A girl rushed over to help him, her eyes wide with concern. "Ryan, are you okay?" Lainey asked, glancing up at her with surprise.

"Who's that?" Ryan asked, still staring at Beth.

Lainey shrugged, "Whoever she is, that was pretty rude of her."

Meanwhile, across the courtyard, a group of football players were in deep discussion; their leader, Alex, the star quarterback, stood near the fountain. Tall and built like a wall, he commanded a presence that turned heads. His gaze sharpened as it landed on Beth, intrigued and mildly amused by her bold entrance.

As Beth strode toward him, confidence radiated from her. She leaned casually against the fountain, flashing a charming smile. "Hey there," she greeted. "I'm Beth. New here."

Alex, caught off guard for a moment, returned her smile with a hint of intrigue. "I'm Alex. Senior."

Beth's eyes sparkled with mischief. "You play football?"

He nodded, his expression steady, "Quarterback."

She glared at him playfully, her eyes hinting a challenge.

Alex's demeanor shifted slightly as he noticed.

Beth's heart raced, a thrill coursing through her as she gauged the tension.

She laughed lightly, but beneath her bravado, she felt a flicker of uncertainty.

The bell rang again as he turned away, leaving Beth standing at the fountain, a swirl of emotions in her chest.

He looked back at her, "Beth, right? Try not to make any enemies on your first day.

Chapter 3
Homeroom

Beth settled into her seat, her heart still racing. The whispers trickled down to a murmur, but the cacophony of judgment lingered in the air like a thick fog. Her fingers brushed against the smooth surface of her desk, grounding her in this moment even as she felt the weight of their gazes.

She tuned in as Mr. Johnson began calling names, his voice methodical and steady. Each response from her classmates was met with an indifferent nod or casual glance from him, but she could sense that their attention was divided; it rested squarely on her.

"Ryan Andrews," Mr. Johnson called, and a lanky boy in the back shot his hand up, a lazy grin lighting up his face. "Here," he replied, feigning nonchalance, but his eyes flickered toward Beth for a brief moment, an eyebrow arched in curiosity, realizing that he had recognized her from earlier.

♥

Beth fought the urge to blush under the scrutiny. She kept her composure, squared her shoulders, and fixed her gaze forward. Each name called elicited various reactions—some giggles, some whispers—an unsettling rhythm she quickly grew tired of. The whispers built again as Mr. Johnson continued.

"Arnold Daniels?"

As Mr. Johnson worked through the names, Beth's mind churned. She wondered if anyone would be friendlier than her classmates had been thus far. It seemed like everyone had a stake in the rumor mill, and the thought made her stomach churn. Did they know what she had done?

"And finally, Beth Harper?"

"Here," she replied, forcing a steadiness into her voice. Once again, all eyes were on her. A whispered exchange flickered between Samantha and her friends, creating a palpable tension that Beth could almost taste.

But the atmosphere remained tense—if anything, it grew more charged. "Today, we're going to discuss social dynamics in history," he said, his tone brimming with enthusiasm. "I think it's important we understand how our past wields power over our present."

As he spoke, Beth felt the implications of his words sharpen. Were they discussing social dynamics? Did that mean the rumors about her weren't just idle chatter? She tried to focus on the lesson, jotting down notes on the eras of struggle and triumph Mr. Johnson detailed, but it was hard to concentrate when the feeling of eyes boring into her back was an ever-present distraction.

"Class, I want you to write an essay about your own experiences within social dynamics. Think about times you felt welcomed or ostracized, and how those experiences shaped your perspective." Mr. Johnson's directive was met with a mixture of groans and reluctant nods—yet his eyes cut through the noise and landed firmly on Beth.

Her heart leapt into her throat, and for a moment, time seemed to stand still. How could she possibly open up about her experiences when she felt so bare? The idea sent her mind spinning. What could she reveal to him that wouldn't draw more scrutiny? Maybe she could make an early ally, or maybe he'd just get her in trouble.

Taking a deep breath, Beth steeled herself. The words slowly formed in her mind, coming together into a story she was ready to share. She glanced at her classmates' faces, unsure how much to reveal, but a feeling of empowerment washed over her.

"It's due Monday," Mr. Johnson stated as the bell rang.

As the bell rang, a cacophony of chatter erupted in the classroom, students rushing to the door and jostling for position in the narrow hallway. Mr. Johnson stood at the front, guiding the students with a practiced ease.

"Beth," he said, catching her gaze just as she began to rise from her seat. "Could you stay behind for a moment? I'd like to have a quick chat."

The bustle of students faded as the door clicked shut behind the last of her classmates. Beth sat back down, her heart thudding in her chest. Mr. Johnson leaned against his desk, his salt-and-pepper hair catching the faint sunlight streaming through the window.

"So, how are you fitting in?" he asked, genuine concern etching lines on his face.

♥

Beth felt a knot tighten in her throat as the question stirred old wounds she had hoped to leave behind. She glanced down at her hands, clenched tightly, as if they could hold back her uncertainty. "Well, when I was at my last school, I..." she began, her voice shaky but growing steadier, "didn't really fit in. I guess I was kind of a target for..." She hesitated, the weight of memories pressing down on her—each one filled with laughter that didn't include her and the gossip that did. The memory of the stares pierced like arrows.

Her mind raced, conjuring images of isolation—lunches spent alone, eye rolls exchanged behind her back, and the whispering echoes of "weird" ringing in her ears. Swallowing hard, she fought to keep her composure, grappling with the vulnerability that lay bare before her teacher.

But as she looked up, she saw Mr. Johnson listening intently, not just as an authority figure but as someone genuinely invested in her well-being. A flicker of defiance ignited deep within her as she wrestled with her fears.

A wave of silence washed over her face—silent but charged, yet shifting. Beth noticed his expression soften, a flicker of understanding sparking in his eyes.

For the first time since entering the classroom, something in Beth's chest unclenched. Maybe, just maybe, she could carve out her place in this new territory after all.

Chapter 4

An Intriguing Invitation

The cafeteria at Oakridge was a cavernous hall of polished linoleum and high-stakes social maneuvering. For Beth, it was the ultimate test. It was one thing to blend into a crowd of hundreds at a homecoming game; it was quite another to navigate the daylight reality of her first official day as a transfer student.

The air was thick with the smell of over-cooked pizza and the deafening roar of six hundred simultaneous conversations. Beth gripped her tray—standard-issue plastic that felt like a shield—and scanned the room. She didn't look for an empty seat; she looked for a specific jersey.

She found him at the center table, the "Golden Table," situated directly under the skylight where the afternoon sun seemed to bless them with a natural shine. Alex was leaning back in his chair, one arm draped over the empty seat next to him, looking less like a student and more like the sovereign ruler of the room.

Beth took a breath, smoothed her hair, and threaded her way through the throng of underclassmen. She stopped just behind him, close enough to smell the faint scent of cedarwood and laundry detergent that clung to his jacket.

"Hey, look who it is," she said, pitching her voice to be heard over the surrounding chatter without sounding like she was trying too hard.

Alex turned, his movements slow and deliberate. When his eyes landed on her, the distracted mask he wore for his teammates fell away, replaced by a flicker of genuine recognition. A slow, lopsided smirk pulled at the corner of his mouth.

"Hey! If it isn't the new girl," he said, shifting his weight so he was fully facing her. "I wasn't sure if you were a ghost or just a dream. Surviving the first-day gauntlet?"

"Barely," Beth replied, offering a playful, weary tilt of her head. "I've been asked for my hall pass three times, and I still haven't found the chemistry lab. I think this school was designed as a labyrinth."

Alex chuckled, a low sound that vibrated under the noise of the room. "It gets easier." He paused, his gaze lingering on her for a moment before he pushed the chair back and gestured for her to sit. "Join us."

"This is the infamous new girl?" the guy across from them joked.

"Infamous?" she inquired, "What did you hear?"

"Oh, you know, the usual," another boy stung.

"Guys, stop," Alex said, and what Alex said went.

"Are you going to Patty's pool party?" Jake asked.

"Of course she is, bro... Beth, this is my best friend Jake," he told her. "We've been friends since I can remember... You are coming right?"

"I don't know, bro, Patty still hasn't forgiven you for the breakup, remember?"

"It'll be fine," Alex assured her, "just come, for me, I know you want to..."

Beth looked at him with a flirtatious glitter in her eye. "Oh? Are you inviting me? Whose party is it?"

The tables' attention shifted to the far end of the cafeteria, where Patricia Patrick sat surrounded by a flock of cheerleaders.

"Look," Alex said, leaning in a little closer, "tomorrow is Saturday. We're celebrating the Homecoming win. Patty's throwing a pool party at her place. Her parents are always out on vacation anyway."

"Are you sure? It seems like you two have some history."

"Don't worry about it," Alex's eyes glittered at her as if to say, 'Just do it anyway.'

Beth glanced over at Patricia. The Queen looked radiant even in the harsh fluorescent lighting, sipping from a glass bottle of sparkling water.

Beth stopped for a moment, *'So it begins...'* she thought, then snapped her attention back to him.

"Well, I guess I have to, seeing that your invitations seem to be of official royal decree, my king," her eyebrows arched.

"Consider it a personal invite," Alex said, his voice dropping to a more intimate register. "You should definitely be there. It's an Oakridge staple—half the school will be trying to crash, but I'll make sure you're on the right side of the gate. Besides," he added with a conspiratorial wink, "Patty's parents are beyond loaded, and they're always off on vacation in the Hamptons or Cabo. The house is basically ours for the weekend."

The invitation hung in the air, heavy with the promise of belonging. Beth felt a rush of adrenaline—the plan was working. She wasn't just a face in the crowd anymore; she was being pulled into the sun's orbit.

Beth snapped back to reality, drawn to a beautiful girl who suddenly appeared behind the table. Her striking black hair contrasted with her pale skin and gold cheer outfit, but what stood out most were her piercing dark green eyes, fixed directly on Beth.

She ignored the boys entirely, her eyes steadily locked onto Beth with a predatory kind of friendliness.

"Alex, you're hogging her," Samantha chirped, "I just **have** to meet the new girl properly. Come with us, sweetie."

Beth felt the table go quiet. She sensed the underlying tension, the invisible line drawn between the players and the squad. She stood up, smoothing her jacket to hide a flash of nerves.

As she stepped away, Alex leaned back, his eyes narrowing slightly as he looked up at her. "So you're coming right?" he asked, his voice powered through the noise of the food hall.

"Yeah, uh, here, text me the details," Beth replied, offering a quick, reassuring smile, handing him her phone before Samantha whisked her away toward a circular booth in the corner.

"I'm Samantha, by the way, leader of the cheer squad," the girl said, sliding into the vinyl seat and gesturing for Beth to join the circle of pom-poms and perfectly winged eyeliner.

Beth sat, her internal alarm bells ringing. She was slightly concerned that it might be a setup, a classic "mean girl" interrogation to sniff out an outsider, but she straightened her posture. *'Two can play that game,'* she thought.

"So, spill," one of the other cheerleaders leaned in, propping her chin on her hand. "Where did you transfer from? We haven't seen a new face in Oakridge for years."

The question was a landmine. If she mentioned Northwood, the rival school across the county, the hospitality would evaporate instantly. Beth didn't miss a beat, wiggling through a lie about being from a distant town three hours north—a place small enough that no one would likely have cousins there. She kept the details vague, her voice steady, successfully masking the truth to avoid the inevitable fallout of being the "enemy" in their midst.

Chapter 5

Football Practice

As the sun began to dip below the horizon, casting a golden hue over the field, Alex's focus was on the practice drills. He was the star quarterback, always intent on perfecting each throw. However, the chatter of the cheerleaders on the sidelines kept drifting into his consciousness.

"Have you heard about the new girl?" one cheerleader gossiped, twirling a lock of hair. "They say she was expelled for being... You know, a slut."

Another one snickered in response. "Yeah, can you believe it? I hope she doesn't mess up our good vibes here at Oakridge."

♥

Alex's brow furrowed as he threw a perfect spiral to a receiver. *Who was this new girl, Beth? Why was she being judged before anyone even knew her?*

He glanced over at the sideline, trying to catch a glimpse of the cheerleaders.

Alex exhaled sharply, wiping sweat from his brow before pulling off his helmet. The moment he did, a hush fell over the cheerleaders for the briefest second—then erupted into giggles and exaggerated poses as he neared them.

"Hey, Alex!" one chirped, flipping her ponytail over her shoulder. "Looking sharp out there today."

Another leaned in with a teasing grin. "Tough practice, or are you just that smooth?"

Alex smirked, shaking his head as he toweled off. "It's chirpier than usual over here. What's all the gossip?"

The first cheerleader perked up. "Oh, just some stuff about that new girl. Beth something? Apparently, her last school kicked her out for reasons—that's the gossip." She wiggled her eyebrows at him.

"And we're just saying," the second girl cut in, "Oakridge has standards. We don't need **her** kind messing up the—"

Alex chuckled dryly, cutting her off. "So let me get this straight. You barely even talked to her, no one here's even really gotten to know her yet, but you're already writing her off with rumors?" He shrugged, feigning nonchalance, but there was an edge in his tone. "Sounds like you're more worried about 'standards' than actually knowing the person behind the rumors."

The girls blinked, exchanging glances. One opened her mouth to protest, but Alex was already walking away, tossing a final remark over his shoulder. "Maybe give her a chance before you decide who she is."

Their laughter stuttered into awkward silence as he left them behind, curiosity flickering in the back of his mind. Who was Beth, really?

♥

As the final bell rang, an excited hum filled the hallways of Oakridge High. Whispers began to ripple through the crowd like a wave, each student eager to share the latest gossip. It was common knowledge by now that something unusual had happened that morning—something involving the new student, Beth Harper.

"Did you hear? She's already causing a scene!" Sarah, the ever-enthusiastic sophomore, exclaimed to her friends as they gathered by their lockers.

"Yeah, I heard she showed up late to class, and Mr. Hargrove went off on her," Tom chimed in, leaning against a nearby locker, his face lit up with intrigue.

"No way! That's not the half of it," another student joined the fray. "I overheard in the cafeteria that she had a huge fight with some upperclassman. They say she stood her ground, though!"

Word spread quickly through the hallways, every version becoming more exaggerated than the last. By the time lunch rolled around, Beth was rumored to have defeated not just one but a small army of bullies.

"Rumor has it she had them all backing down, begging for mercy!" another girl laughed, tossing her hair back dramatically while a group giggled around her.

As the rumors spread, they took on a life of their own. By the end of the school day, Beth was no longer just the new girl; she was a legend in the making, a figure shrouded in mystery and the allure of rebellion.

But amidst the noise and chaos, Beth remained blissfully unaware. Unbeknownst to her, the storm of gossip swirling would soon collide with her quiet existence, setting the stage for a drama that would captivate the entire school.

Chapter 6

Patty's Pool Party

The sun was warm, as if its only priority was to provide heat for Patty's sprawling backyard, turning the pool water into a hot liquid gold. Music thumped from speakers hidden in the landscaping, laughter and splashing echoed everywhere, and the smell of chlorine mixed with sunscreen and spilled beer hung thick in the air.

Beth, still carrying that shiny new-girl aura, had already charmed half the school and repulsed the rest. She set out to gain the favor of the cheer squad with her easy confidence and cool demeanor. The football guys had taken to calling her "Hollywood" because of the way she moved—like she knew exactly where every eye was landing.

Alex noticed her walk in and called her over.

He didn't yell; he just caught her eye and gestured with a slight tilt of his head toward the inner circle of the team standing around a small bonfire.

"It's Beth, right?" one of the guys asked, a linebacker whose name she didn't know yet.

"Yeah," she said, seizing the opportunity to position herself closer. She moved closer to Alex, pretending as if it were only to warm her hands by the fire.

The bass of the music thumped in the background as she engaged in small talk, laughing at jokes and offering compliments about the game.

"Were you at the game?" someone asked. "When did you transfer?"

Beth stopped for a moment, then proceeded to lie, "No," she said, "I transferred last week, but I didn't know about the game."

As the party wore on, the atmosphere grew ever livelier in conjunction with the setting of the sun, and likewise, Beth noticed Alex's guarded demeanor starting to soften with every sip of beer. The heavy weight of the "Homecoming King" persona seemed to lift as the crowd's attention shifted toward a drinking game across the yard. He stopped performing the role of the captain and started looking restless. His eyes wandered away from the flickering flames toward the pool.

Beth noticed him slip away from the group, without a word, and slide down to dip his feet back into the water. He sat alone on the concrete lip of the deep end; the blue pool lights behind his legs cast a ghostly glow across the water.

She seized the chance to be alone with him and found herself wandering over to sit with him.

"Are you getting in?" he asked, watching her shift down to take a seat.

"Maybe later."

"Good idea," red cup in hand, he took another sip.

His hair was dark and slick from swimming earlier, droplets still clinging to his shoulders.

"Thanks for inviting me," she said, voice low enough that it felt private even with thirty people around. "I was starting to think I'd be eating lunch alone as the outcast, you know, being the new girl, n' all."

Alex gave her that half-smile he always used when he wasn't sure whether to play it cool or just admit he was already hooked. "Figured you'd fit right in."

He shoved off into the water, "Come on."

She stood up, her bikini the color of ripe cherries, and slowly walked down into the water, again noticing the attention she immediately gained.

She paced through the water and threw her arms around his neck. "It's cold," she shivered. He swung her around, "You didn't have to get in."

She smirked at him and sank under the water. Alex watched as she popped back up, tilting her head sideways. She dusted off the wet strands of blonde hair sprinkled across her shoulder and swiped away the chunks stuck to her neck, then she shook her head quickly as she threw it back.

She again drifted closer until their legs brushed under the surface. "I like fitting in," she murmured. Her fingers found his wrist beneath the water, light at first, then firmer. "Especially with you."

Around them, people were shouting, cannonballing, losing flip-flops—but the space between Alex and Beth had its own gravity now.

The music shifted again, and with it the mood. She didn't know if it made him more sober or more hypnotized, so she planned her attack carefully.

She leaned in first.

Their mouths met, soft, testing, then hungry. Her lips were warm despite the cool water, tasting faintly of cherry ChapStick, and his of a pale beer. Alex's hand slid to the small of her back, pulling her flush against him. She made a small, needy sound against his tongue that sent heat ripping straight through him.

Beth's fingers curled into his hair, tugging just hard enough to make him groan quietly into her mouth. She kissed like she was claiming something—deep, deliberate, no hesitation. Her thighs brushed his hips under the water; he could feel her pulse racing where their bodies pressed.

She broke the kiss just long enough to whisper against his jaw, breath hot, "Come with me."

She didn't wait for an answer. Her hand found his, and she tugged him toward the far side of the pool, up the steps, water streaming off both of them.

A few of the guys hooted when they saw Alex being led away, but Beth didn't even glance back. She just kept that same confident stride, wet footprints darkening the patio tiles.

The bathroom was down a short hallway, the door slightly ajar. She pushed it open, pulled him inside, and kicked it shut behind them.

The lock clicked.

Beth turned, backing him against the sink in one smooth motion. Her hands were already sliding under his soaked T-shirt, nails grazing his stomach. "Been thinking about this since the first time I saw you on the field," she said, voice rougher now. She tugged the shirt up and off, letting it slap wetly to the tile.

Alex caught her wrists gently, just to slow her for a second. "You sure?"

Her gaze was dark, pupils blown, eyes wide. She pressed her whole body against him, hips rolling in a slow, deliberate grind that made his breath hitch. "I've been sure for weeks."

That was all it took.

Alex groaned into her mouth when she wrapped her fingers around him, stroking once, slow and firm from base to tip.

"Fuck, Beth—"

With an evil smile at the way he jerked in her, she cut him off by sinking to her knees. She looked up at him in a drooling daze, her fingers worked the knot of his board shorts, she giggled as they splashed to the floor, his cock flopping into her mouth.

The first touch of her tongue made his head thud back against the mirror. She didn't tease this time; she took him deep right away, lips sealing tight, cheeks hollowing as she sucked. One hand braced on his thigh, the other curled around what her mouth couldn't reach, stroking in perfect rhythm with the slide of her tongue along the underside. Wet heat, pressure, the soft scrape of teeth—just enough to make his hips punch forward involuntarily.

She hummed around him, the vibration ripping a curse out of his throat. Her eyes flicked up, dark and smug, watching every twitch of his face while she worked him faster. Saliva glistened on her lips, dripped down her chin. She didn't care. Neither did he.

He was painfully hard. He watched himself throb with pleasure as she removed her bikini top. She stood up and pressed against him with a hot, condescending breath. Her bikini bottoms fell, feathering slowly to the floor.

Just when he thought he couldn't get any harder, there she stood—more than confidently naked, almost devilishly delighted.

The counter was cold against his back when she pushed him up onto it. She climbed into his lap, knees bracketing his hips, and the first real slide of skin on skin made them both gasp.

Beth set the pace—slow at first, savoring every inch, every catch of breath, every scrape of nails down his shoulders. Then faster. Deeper. The mirror behind them fogged quickly. Her head tipped back, throat exposed, moans spilling out unchecked now.

Alex gripped her hips, thumbs digging in, matching her rhythm until they were both trembling, chasing the same edge.

When she came, it was with his name on her lips—sharp, broken, beautiful.

He followed seconds later, burying his face in her neck, holding her tight as he poured out inside of her.

For a long minute, they just breathed against each other, hearts hammering, skin slick with sweat and pool water.

Beth finally laughed—soft, a little dazed—and kissed the corner of his mouth.

"Welcome to the team, quarterback," she whispered as he pulled out slowly, watching his cock glisten with arousal.

Beth's head dropped forward, blonde hair swinging, knuckles white on the counter. "Fuck—yes..."

Alex grinned against her shoulder.

He could definitely get used to this.

Chapter 7

Not So Cinderella

Alex and Beth left the bathroom and found their way back into the party. The air in the hallway was cooler, but as they stepped back into the main room, the bass-heavy music hit them again.

As the night progressed, the effects of alcohol began to loosen inhibitions. Beth, fueled by liquid courage, attempted to draw Alex into a more personal conversation, leaning closer to him than necessary to be heard over the speakers. The football players nearby exchanged glances, their camaraderie evident as they navigated the social dynamics of the party, watching their captain with a mix of amusement and curiosity.

♥

Just when Beth thought she was making headway, digging for something deeper beneath his 'King' persona, Alex's eyes hardened with a flash of sharp clarity that cut through his relaxed state—a warning in their depths as if to say, 'You're playing a dangerous game, Beth.' It was the look of someone who knew she was hiding something too, even if he couldn't name it yet.

Beth, momentarily caught off guard by the intensity of his stare, quickly recovered with a dizzying smile. "I'm just here to have a good time, Alex."

He nodded, a hint of skepticism in his gaze. "We'll see."

As the night unfolded, Beth found herself entangled in the web of high school drama. Friendships were forged over shared drinks, alliances formed in the kitchen, and secrets shared under the veil of a chaotic, alcohol-fueled night. For Beth, though, the line between 'playing a part' and reality began to blur.

♥

Driven by a restless need to keep up appearances, she accepted every red solo cup pushed her way, the burning liquid dulling the sharp edges of her plan. The music became a physical weight, pulsing through the floorboards until she felt she had to escape the crush of bodies. She began to wander, her footsteps heavy and uncoordinated as she drifted away from the kitchen. She bypassed a group of laughing freshmen and slipped into the darker, quieter hallway of the massive estate and stumbled into a mercifully empty parlor room near the entrance.

The whole scene made her head throb, but she did notice that the school's attention wasn't on her for once, leaving her to sit alone inside the large parlor. She glared at Alex across the way in the living room through the window of the fireplace with an intensity only matched by the crackling of the fire.

She seemed to be all but forgotten now; the only regard she garnered was from the fire, as it seemingly watched her back. The room was spinning slightly and even a bit wavy, but then a sharp clarity settled over her. She took another gulp of her drink. Admittedly, the 'drunk girl act' had started to fade into the real thing, but despite the slipping sobriety, she still had a job to do.

♥

She stood up from the bench and smoothed her hair in the vanity mirror.

It was time for Operation Sabotage: Beth set out to find Patty.

She found the Homecoming Queen near the kitchen, surrounded by a smaller, more elite circle than the one scattered around the backyard. Patty was nursing a drink, looking bored with the very party she was supposed to be hosting. Beth took a deep breath and stepped into her line of sight.

"Hey, Patricia, right? I just wanted to find you and say thanks for letting me come tonight," Beth said, her voice pitched with a perfect mix of sweetness and New-Girl nerves. "I really wanted to meet you."

Patricia looked Beth up and down, her eyes scanning for flaws like a laser. "Aren't you the new girl?" she asked, her tone dripping with a practiced, icy indifference. "I didn't expect you to be here. Who invited you, anyway?"

"Alex did," Beth replied simply.

The reaction was instantaneous. Patricia's hand tightened around her cup, and her lip curled in a flicker of genuine revulsion. She looked disgusted with Alex—the kind of look reserved only for an ex-boyfriend who had overstepped a boundary.

"Of course he did," Patricia muttered, rolling her eyes toward the ceiling. "Typical."

Beth maintained her innocent expression, but internally, she was grinning. She was secretly already sure of their messy breakup, and she knew exactly how much mentioning his name would sting. Patricia launched into a mini-rant about Alex's 'lack of taste.' Beth nodded sympathetically, leaning in as if they were already confidantes. She wasn't just making a friend; she was building a bridge she intended to burn.

She was officially in, and the sabotage had begun.

♥

With Patricia finally occupied by a new admirer, Beth drifted back toward the center of the room. The adrenaline of her successful manipulation began to fade, replaced by the heavy, creeping warmth of the drinks she'd been using as props. To celebrate her victory over the Queen Bee, she found herself at the makeshift bar again, tipping back a mixture that burned much harder than the last. The house seemed to tilt slightly as the bass dropped, the rhythm of the party becoming a frantic, blurred heartbeat that she could no longer ignore. She lost track of where Patricia went, and more importantly, she lost track of her own restraint.

Chapter 8

Not So Sleeping Beauty

The drinks caught up to her all at once. Her laughter became too loud, her steps too heavy. She found herself dancing on a coffee table, nearly toppling over a lamp, before a pair of strong hands caught her by the waist. She was making a complete fool of herself, the 'mysterious new girl' facade crumbling into a messy, drunken haze.

"Okay, that's enough," Alex's voice was firm, cutting through her fog.

He didn't make a scene. He simply steered her through the crowd, ignoring the whistles from his teammates, and led her up the stairs to a quiet guest bedroom. He sat her down on the edge of the duvet, the muffled thumping of the party vibrating through the floorboards.

Feeling the sudden rush of being alone with him, Beth reached out, her fingers fumbling with the collar of his shirt. She pulled herself closer, her breath smelling of soda and cheap vodka as she tried to bridge the gap between them, her intentions written clearly in her glazed eyes.

Alex gently but firmly caught her wrists, holding her back. "Stop," he said softly, his voice grounded and devoid of any playfulness. "You're too drunk, Beth. You aren't going to want this tomorrow."

He stood up, pulling a blanket from the foot of the bed and tossing it over her lap.

"Go to bed, Beth," he demanded, but she wasn't having it.

She stood up quickly in a haze, swaying a little on unsteady legs, the room tilting just enough to make her giggle at nothing in particular. Her cheeks were flushed deeper than any amount of drinking could explain alone. Her eyes were glassy and bright, with a reckless sparkle.

"Bed. Now," she announced to the room like there were more people than just him and her in it. Grabbing fistfuls of his shirt and yanking him down with more enthusiasm than coordination, he reluctantly let her pull him. They both half-laughingly tumbled onto the mattress in a tangle of limbs.

She rolled on top of him first, straddling his hips with exaggerated triumph, then—without warning—spun around so her back was to him. The movement was clumsy, almost comical; she nearly toppled sideways, catching herself on his thighs with a breathless "whoops" that dissolved into another giggle.

"Okay, okay, watch this," she said, voice thick and playful, slurring just enough to make every word feel like a secret. She reached for the hem of her top, fingers fumbling at the fabric like it had personally offended her. She tugged it up slowly—too slowly—then got stuck halfway, arms tangled overhead, bra straps twisted, the shirt bunched around her face.

"Help," she mumbled through cotton, muffled and laughing at herself. "Or don't. This is sexy, right?"

He snorted, sitting up enough to gently free her arms. The shirt finally came off, hair wild and staticky, cheeks even redder now. She tossed it somewhere behind her—missing the floor entirely—and it landed on the lamp instead, casting a soft, ridiculous glow.

Next came the bra. She reached back, fingers missing the clasp twice before she huffed dramatically. "Stupid thing," she muttered, twisting awkwardly. Finally, it gave; she shrugged the straps down her shoulders with theatrical slowness, letting the cups fall forward one at a time like she was revealing state secrets. Her breasts spilled free, nipples already tight from the cool air and the way his eyes hadn't left her once.

She arched her back, then—more dramatic than graceful—pushed her ass back toward him while still half-straddling his lap. The motion was wobbly, tipsy, but deliberate in its flirtation; she rolled her hips once, twice, grinding back against the growing hardness beneath his jeans with a pleased little hum.

Her hands went to the waist of her tights next, pulling them down her thighs in awkward, hopping increments until she could kick them off one leg at a time.

Now in just panties—black lace already damp at the center—she turned again, clumsy and eager, so her back was fully to him. She braced both hands on the edge of the bed, arched deeply, ass pressing back against his cock through the denim he still wore. She rolled, slow and deliberate—or as deliberate as her current state allowed—hips swaying in uneven circles, giggling every time she almost lost her balance.

The room seemed to glow softer around her: flushed cheeks, parted lips still curved in a drunk, giddy smile, breasts rising and falling with each uneven breath.

Alex's hands found her hips, thumbs digging into soft flesh to steady her. She whimpered at the contact, pushing back harder, trying to chase more friction.

"Take these off," she demanded, as she had already nearly gotten them off of him somehow.

He just laughed low in amazement—she was a beautiful, awkward, gloriously drunk mess—and he was pretty gone too.

Bracing both hands on the edge, she arched—ass pressing back against his cock, rolling, slow and deliberate. The room seemed to illuminate around her. Her flushed cheeks, parted lips, the way her chest rose and fell with each breath, nipples tight and eager.

Alex's hands found her hips, thumbs digging into soft flesh. He dragged the head of his cock through her folds—slick, swollen, dripping—and she whimpered, pushing back, trying to take him.

He reached around, fingers finding her clit—swollen, slippery—and circled fast, matching the rhythm of his hips. She jerked, inner walls clamping down so tight he nearly lost it right then.

"Look," he growled against her ear. "Look at us."

She lifted her head.

Their eyes locked in the mirror across the room—hers glazed with desperation, his dark with hunger. He watched her watch them: the way her breasts bounced with each thrust, the flex of his forearms as he held her, the stretch of her body taking every inch.

Beth's moans turned broken, high. "I'm—oh god—I'm gonna—"

He pinched her clit lightly, rolled it between finger and thumb.

She shattered.

Her whole body seized—back arching, thighs shaking, a raw, keening cry tearing from her throat. She pulsed around him, rhythmic and hard, milking him so fiercely he could barely move.

He fucked her through it anyway, shorter, sharper strokes, drawing it out until she was whimpering.

Only then did he let himself go.

They stayed like that for a long second—panting, slick with sweat, hearts hammering against ribs.

Beth finally laughed, low and wrecked. She reached back, threading fingers through his damp hair, tugging him down for a lazy, open-mouthed kiss over her shoulder.

"Still think I fit in?" she murmured against his lips.

Alex huffed a laugh, still inside her, softening slowly. "Yeah," he said, voice rough. "You fit just fine."

She squeezed around him one last teasing time, making him hiss, then eased forward so he slipped free. A slow trickle of their combined release slid down her inner thigh, but she didn't bother cleaning it up—just turned, kissed him again, and thumped her head onto the pillow.

Chapter 9
Wake Up, Whore

The heavy, thumping bass of the night had finally bled out into a hollow silence, leaving the house smelling of stale beer and dying embers.

Beth had only just settled into the heavy blankets, her mind finally drifting toward a much-needed blackout, when the peace was shattered.

The party slowed as the early mornings passed, dawn peeking through the window in thin, dusty needles of light. Just as she felt the pull of unconsciousness and shut her eyes to sleep, the light from the hallway blinded her as the door swung open violently.

The heavy oak door slammed against the stopper with a crack that sounded like a gunshot. Beth bolted upright, her heart hammering against her ribs, her vision swimming in the sudden, harsh glare of the hallway lights.

Standing in the doorway, framed by the golden glow like a vengeful specter, was Patricia. Her perfect hair was slightly disheveled from the long night, and her makeup was smudged, but her eyes were sharp with a lethal, freezing fury.

She didn't say a word at first. She just stared at the scene: Beth, the 'new girl' she'd just started to trust, and Alex, the ex-boyfriend she claimed to despise, occupying the same tangled mess of sheets and pillows.

"I knew you were full of it," Patty spat, her voice a jagged whisper that sliced through the morning air. "But this? This is low, even for a transfer."

Beside Beth, Alex stirred, shielding his eyes from the light with a groan, completely unaware that the bridge Beth had been building was currently going up in flames right in front of them.

The hallway behind Patty suddenly filled with muffled voices and shuffling footsteps—half the partygoers who'd been crashing in the living room or passed out on couches had been roused by the door slam and the rising pitch of her voice. A few heads poked around the doorframe: sleepy-eyed, hungover, but suddenly very awake.

"Patty, what the hell?" Alex muttered, rubbing his face.

Beth, clutching the sheet to her chest, hair a wreck, skin still flushed from everything that had happened hours earlier; Alex, blinking groggily beside her, shirtless and clearly just woken up.

Patty didn't wait for backup. She stormed forward, bare feet slapping the hardwood, fury propelling her like a missile.

"Get the fuck out of my house," she hissed at Beth, voice cracking on the last word. She lunged for the edge of the sheet, yanking hard.

Beth yelped, scrambling to hold on. The fabric twisted in her fists as she tried to stay covered, knees drawn up, one arm clamped across her breasts while the other death-gripped the corner of the comforter. "Patty—stop—"

The sheet slipped an inch, then another. Cold air hit Beth's bare thigh; she squeaked and yanked it back up, cheeks burning hotter than the alcohol still lingering in her system. "This isn't—fuck—can we not do this right now?"

Patty's fingers clawed at the bedding, trying to rip it away completely. "You don't get to play innocent! You knew exactly what you were doing, you little—"

"Enough!" Alex barked, finally fully awake. He sat up fast, throwing an arm across Beth's front like a shield, blocking Patty's reach. "Back off, Patty. Now!"

♥

Patty froze, chest heaving, eyes darting between them. Tears shimmered at the edges of her rage—hurt, betrayal, the kind that had been simmering for months and finally boiled over.

"You're seriously defending her?" she spat at him. "After everything?"

Another girl stepped forward cautiously, hands raised. "Patty, babe, come on. Let's go downstairs. You're drunk, we're all wrecked. This doesn't have to—"

"I'm not drunk," Patty snapped, though the slur in her words said otherwise. She tried one more vicious tug at the sheet; Beth held fast, the fabric straining between them like a rope in a tug-of-war.

Patty stood there trembling, glaring down at Beth with so much venom it felt physical.

"You're not welcome here anymore," she said, low and venomous. "Either of you."

Beth swallowed hard, still clutching the sheet like a lifeline, heart slamming against her ribs. "Patty, I didn't mean to—"

"Save it." Patty turned on her heel, shoving past the evermore forming crowd. The others parted for her like she was radioactive. She disappeared down the hallway, footsteps echoing, followed a second later by the crash of another door slamming somewhere deeper in the house.

Silence fell, thick and awkward.

Alex exhaled slowly, glancing at Beth with something like sympathy mixed with secondhand embarrassment. "You okay?"

Beth let out a shaky laugh that sounded more like a sob. "Define okay."

Alex rubbed a hand over his face, then reached for Beth's shoulder, squeezing gently. "She'll cool off. She always does."

Beth pulled the sheet tighter around herself, suddenly hyper-aware of how naked she was under the thin cotton, how exposed she felt with half a dozen hungover witnesses still lingering in the doorway.

"I think I should go," she said quietly.

Alex's grip tightened. "Uh... maybe everyone else should go..."

The small crowd shuffled backward, muttering apologies and gossip as they dispersed.

The room settled into a bruised quiet.

Outside the door, the house groaned back to life—footsteps, low voices, the distant clink of coffee mugs. The night was officially over.

And the fallout had only just begun.

Chapter 10

Manic Monday

Beth had spent the entire weekend holed up in her room, phone on silent except for the handful of texts from Alex that kept her from spiraling completely:

> You okay?

> Patty is s still pissed.

Give her time.

Miss your face.

She'd replied to each one—short, careful, trying to sound casual even though her stomach was in knots. Every time she closed her eyes, she replayed the door slamming open, Patty's venom, the way half the party had seen her naked and clutching a sheet like it was armor.

Monday morning came too fast.

Her phone buzzed insistently at 6:15, then again at 6:20, and finally a third time at 6:30 when she finally slapped it silent. She lay there for another full minute, staring at the ceiling of her room, the faint glow of streetlights seeping through the blinds in thin, pale stripes. Her body felt heavy, like the weekend's anxiety had settled into her bones.

She dragged herself upright, peeled off the oversized tee she'd slept in—cotton worn soft from too many washes, the hem frayed where it had caught on the dresser drawer one too many times—and let it drop to the floor in a careless heap. Her skin prickled in the cool air of the room; goosebumps rose along her arms and the curve of her lower back.

She padded barefoot slowly into the bathroom, the tile cold against the soles of her feet, each step deliberate, almost reluctant. The door clicked shut behind her. She twisted the lock with a small, decisive snick—more habit than necessity—and exhaled, the sound loud in the quiet space.

She stood for a moment in nothing but her panties, staring in the mirror with a growing evil grin. Her hair tangled and sleep-mussed, faint shadows under her eyes, the constellation of small bruises blooming across her collarbone and the inner curve of one breast like dark violet fingerprints. She looked away quickly, not ready to catalog the evidence of Friday night. Reaching back, she hooked her thumbs into the waistband. The elastic had left faint pink lines across her hips overnight. She slid them down slowly—first over the gentle flare of her hips, then past the dip of her waist, letting the fabric drag along the tops of her thighs, then stepped out of them one foot at a time.

She turned to face the shower, bearing it her nakedness. She reached in and twisted the shower knob to nearly scalding. The pipes groaned once, then water burst out in a hard, hot rush. Steam rose almost immediately, curling thick and white, fogging the small mirror above the sink outside the curtain in soft, blurring waves.

Beth stepped under the spray.

The heat hit her like a slap—first shocking, then enveloping. She gasped softly as it cascaded over her shoulders, down the long plane of her back, tracing the shallow dip of her spine before spilling over the curves of her ass. Water plastered her hair to her neck in dark, heavy ropes almost instantly. She tilted her head forward, letting the pounding stream hammer directly against the nape of her neck, the base of her skull, the tight knot between her shoulder blades that hadn't loosened since Saturday morning.

Her arms hung loose at her sides for a long moment, palms open, fingers twitching as the heat worked its way in. Rivulets raced down her breasts, beading briefly on her nipples before sliding lower—over the soft curve of her stomach, between her thighs, following the sensitive crease where leg met body. She shifted her weight, parting her feet slightly, and the water found new paths, warm and insistent, sluicing over every inch of exposed skin.

She closed her eyes.

The steam thickened around her, turning the small stall into a warm, private cocoon. For the first time in forty-eight hours, the noise in her head—the looping replay of Patty's voice, the imagined whispers in hallways she hadn't even walked yet—dulled to a low, distant hum beneath the steady roar of the shower.

She stayed like that for minutes, simply breathing in the heat, letting it strip away the top layer of tension the way it stripped away the faint stickiness of sleep sweat. Her skin flushed deep pink from neck to thighs, every pore open, every nerve singing under the relentless downpour.

She pressed her palms flat against the tile wall, letting the water sheet down her back in hot rivers.

Slowly, almost without deciding to, one hand slid down her stomach. She traced the faint red lines the sheet had left across her hip from when she'd clutched it so desperately. Lower. The soft swell of her mound. She exhaled shakily.

Her fingers parted her folds—still a little tender from Friday night—and found the slick heat waiting there. She was surprised by how ready her body was, how quickly it responded even when her mind was a storm. She circled her clit once, slow, testing. A small, involuntary sound slipped out, swallowed by the rush of water.

She leaned her forehead against her forearm braced on the wall, the other hand sliding up to cup her breast. Her nipple pebbled instantly under her thumb; she pinched lightly, remembering the way Alex's mouth had closed over it, the scrape of his teeth. Her hips rocked forward into her own hand.

The rhythm built gradually—lazy at first, then deeper, more insistent. She slipped two fingers inside herself, curling them the way he had, pressing against that spot that made her thighs tremble. Water streamed over her knuckles, warm and relentless. Her breath came in short, ragged bursts.

She pictured his face—dark eyes locked on hers in the mirror, the flex of his jaw when he came, the low growl of her name against her throat. Then Patty's voice cut through the memory like glass: *'I knew you were full of it.'*

She let out an excited whimper, full of frustration and need. She sped up, thumb working tight circles over her clit while her fingers thrust in shallow, desperate strokes. Her knees shook. The coil in her belly pulled tighter and tighter until it snapped.

She instantly fell to her knees and came violently with a deep depravity of adversarial lust. Her forehead pressed hard against her arm, thighs clamping around her hand as her inner walls pulsed in slow, heavy waves. The release rolled through her in long, shuddering aftershocks, leaving her boneless against the tile.

For several heartbeats, she just breathed—deep, deliberate—letting the water rinse away the evidence, the tension, some of the shame. Not all of it. Never all of it. But enough that she could stand upright again.

She stayed under the spray until it started to run cold, then shut off the tap with a decisive twist.

Back in her room, towel wrapped around her body, she moved slowly, deliberately, like she was putting on armor.

She dropped the towel and stood naked in front of the small mirror on the back of her door.

She pulled on soft cotton boyshorts first—black, simple, no lace today. Then a plain white bralette that hugged without pushing up, the thin straps barely visible under clothes. Next came the jeans: dark wash, high-waisted, fitted enough to feel put-together but loose enough to hide in. She buttoned them with steady fingers.

The hoodie came last—oversized, heather gray, the sleeves long enough to cover her hands if she tugged them down. She rolled the cuffs once anyway, a small gesture of control. Hair still damp, she gathered it into a low, messy bun, securing it with a plain black elastic. No makeup. No jewelry. Just her.

She looked at herself one last time—eyes still tired.

She grabbed her backpack, slung it over one shoulder, and took a deep breath.

The campus waited outside. Rumors waited. Alex waited.

She opened the door and stepped into the hallway, chin up and proud, ready for phase two.

Chapter 11

The Rumors Are True

The first whisper hit her almost immediately as she set foot on the school grounds, not even inside the gate yet.

Two girls she vaguely recognized from one of her classes paused mid-conversation when she walked by. One nudged the other. "That's her, right? The transfer who hooked up with Alex at Patty's party?"

Beth's steps faltered for half a second—long enough for the heat of humiliation to flare bright in her chest, then twist into something sharper, hotter. Something that felt almost like relief.

She stopped.

Turned.

The two girls—both in almost matching hoodies, one with a messy topknot, the other with earbuds dangling from one ear—froze mid-nudge. Their eyes widened in identical, cartoonish surprise when they realized she'd heard every word.

She took two measured steps back toward them, closing the distance until she was close enough to see the faint blush across their cheeks. Almost simultaneously both girls' throats bobbed with nervous swallow.

"Yeah," Beth said, voice low but clear, carrying just far enough that a few other heads nearby turned. "That's me."

One girl blinked rapidly. "We—we weren't—"

"You were," Beth cut in, calm, almost pleasant, "and it's cute how you think whispering makes it less obvious." She tilted her head, studying them like mildly interesting specimens. "So let's do this properly. You've got rumors? Go ahead. Say them to my face."

The other girl opened her mouth, closed it, then glanced at her friend in shock and awe.

Beth smiled—small, sharp, the kind that didn't reach her eyes. "No? Nothing? That's surprising. I've heard the highlights already. Homewrecker, slut, Patty's sloppy seconds." She ticked them off on her fingers like she was reading a grocery list, "Did I miss any good ones?"

Topknot finally found her voice, though it came out thin. "We didn't mean—"

Beth straightened, shoulders back, hoodie sleeves slipping down to reveal the faint purple marks still circling her wrists like bracelets. She didn't bother hiding them.

"You did," Beth said again, softer this time, almost gentle, "so if you're going to keep running your mouths," she continued, tone bright and friendly now, "at least make it interesting. Tell them I screamed his name so loud the neighbors complained. Tell them he fucked me against the mirror so we could both watch. Or—my personal favorite—tell them I came so hard I forgot my own name... Oh, and in case you were wondering," she paused, letting the word hang. "Alex was really, really good."

The girls stared at her—half shock, half unwilling admiration. Topknot's mouth dropped open.

Beth shrugged, casual as anything. "Or don't. Keep it boring and secondhand. Your call." She gave them one last slow once-over, then turned on her heel, hoodie swaying as she walked away, and she didn't look back.

Her heart was hammering so hard she could feel it in her teeth, but the knot in her stomach had loosened for the first time all morning. She wasn't running from this; she's dealt with worse.

She embraced the heat again; the drama is like a warm flame for her to bask in, and the rumor mill is just stoking it for her. She was walking straight into the fire now—and that's the way she liked it.

By the time she reached the science building, the whispers had multiplied. Eyes followed her down the hallway. A guy she'd never spoken to gave her a slow, knowing grin and a little nod like they shared a secret. A girl in a band sweatshirt muttered a giggle under her breath—loud enough to carry—as she passed.

Beth's face burned with anger. She ducked into the first bathroom she saw, locked herself in a stall, pressed her forehead to the cool metal door, and reached for her phone. She texted Alex:

She waited a moment, but he didn't answer.

She slipped into the classroom, hoping that nobody would notice, but the damage was done. Heads turned subtly in her direction. Someone in the row ahead of her opened their group chat and tilted the screen so their friend could see—Beth caught a glimpse of her own name in all caps, followed by a string of fire emojis and a blurry photo that looked suspiciously like the hallway outside Patty's bedroom door.

Mr. Hargrove droned on about synaptic plasticity, but Beth heard none of it. Her skin felt too tight, her pulse too loud. Every cough, every rustle of paper felt like it was aimed at her.

When the lecture finally ended, she bolted—only to run straight into Mia in the hallway.

Mia's expression was unreadable at first: pity, maybe, or something sharper. She stepped in front of Beth, blocking her path.

"Word travels fast," Mia said quietly, "people talk, a lot."

Beth glared at her. "I don't care—"

"I know," Mia cut her off, not unkindly, "but I do, Patty is my best friend. People are filling in the blanks with whatever makes the best story." She hesitated, then added softly, "If you cross her again, I will shut it down, I will end you."

Beth nodded mutely, "You want problems with me, too?"

Mia gave Beth's arm a tight squeeze—then walked away, "Watch your ass, whore."

Chapter 12
Dramaleaders

Beth pushed through the double doors of the gymnasium just after noon. The echo of her sneakers on the polished floor cut through the low hum of gossip and chatter. The cheer squad was practicing in the auxiliary gym at the far end. Glass walls let her see everything: twenty girls in matching navy-and-gold shorts and cropped tanks, hair in high ponytails, moving in sharp, synchronized bursts across the mats. Music thumped from a portable speaker—something fast and bass-heavy.

They were mid-routine, pyramids rising and collapsing with practiced ease.

Beth lingered just outside the door, hoodie still zipped to her chin, arms crossed. She wasn't sure what she was looking for until one girl broke formation, wiped sweat from her brow, and caught sight of her through the glass.

Samantha again—new captain of the squad, notorious for her zero-filter mouth and revered for her ambition—tilted her head, then grinned as she'd just spotted prey that walked right into her trap. She barked something at the squad ("Water break—two minutes!"), then jogged over, pushing the door open with her hip.

"Transfer girl," Samantha said, voice bright and mocking in the way that meant she was already three steps ahead. "It's Beth, right? I heard some interesting news about you. Alex Harding, that's not an easy catch. You went right through the rumor-mill and walked away whistling, huh? I think we should be friends."

Beth didn't flinch. She thought for a moment to puzzle over the game pieces. "I'd like that," she said slyly.

Samantha laughed—short, sharp, approving. She leaned one shoulder against the doorframe, arms folded, sizing Beth up without apology. "Heard you went full scorched-earth in the hallway this morning. Told those two wannabes exactly how loud you scream. Bold. Stupid, maybe. But bold."

Beth shrugged one shoulder, "They started it."

"Yeah, it's quite the play going up against Patty, her being the queen of all rumors after all." Samantha's eyes narrowed, the grin fading into something colder. "She's been gunning for my spot since freshman year. She thinks that because her daddy donates to the school, she should get special treatment. If it wasn't for her, I'd be Homecoming Queen. She's been whispering in ears, turning half the school against anyone who even looks at Alex sideways. Including you."

Beth's pulse kicked. "You're telling me this, why?"

"Because I hate her guts," Samantha said flatly, "and because you just gave her the middle finger in front of witnesses, I like that."

She jerked her chin toward the gym, then looked Beth up and down, "You're a good-looking girl, Beth; fit, pretty, bold, you'd fit right in with us. We've got spots open on the squad. If you show up to practice, you're in, because I said so. If you join, you'd get a lot of leverage around here: uniform, visibility, a squad that's got your back, that goes a long way at Oakridge. Plus—" her smile turned wicked "—you'll be front and center at every game, every event, watching Patty toil, trying to fake her smile and pretend she doesn't want to claw your eyes out."

"What's the catch?" she asked.

Samantha pushed off the doorframe, stepping closer. "You show up to every practice, you learn the routines fast, and you don't flake when it gets hard. Also—" she dropped her voice "—you help us stir up the school to keep us in power. We're in charge around here, not Patty."

Beth let the silence stretch, turning the offer over in her head. This wasn't exactly her scene—too much pep, too much exposure—but exposure was exactly what she needed right now. If the rumors were going to spread anyway, she'd make sure they spread on her terms. Cheer, not so much her sport, but mean-girl politics... absolutely.

The bell rang, leading Beth the perfect opportunity to escape off to P.E. class.

Samantha walked away in silence. She stopped the door from shutting behind her and turned toward Beth, "I'll see you at tryouts?"

Beth nodded.

Chapter 13

More Enemies Than Friends

Beth, already exhausted from a boot-camp-like workout in gym class, let the atmosphere fuel her once again as she stepped into a cafeteria that felt more like a war zone than a food hall.

Trays clattered like artillery shells. Voices overlapped in a relentless barrage—shouts, laughter, the wet smack of food being chewed too loudly, all outshone by fluorescent lights that buzzed over-head, casting everything in a harsh, unforgiving white. Beth cut through it all like a knife through smoke, hoodie up, chin tucked, eyes fixed straight ahead. every few steps, someone lobbed a verbal grenade her way:

"—heard she fucked him in Patty's bed—"
"—slut move, honestly—"
"—Patty's gonna destroy her—"

Still, she didn't flinch, and didn't slow, she knew exactly where Alex was: right in the middle of the damn room like the star of the show.

Beth reached the table in three more strides.

She slammed both palms down on the table so hard that everyone nearby couldn't help but look. The trays jumped, the plastic silverware rattled, and a half-empty soda can tipped, fizzing over the edge.

The noise in the cafeteria didn't drop gradually; it flatlined.

Conversations cut off mid-word. Heads turned in unison. Phones lifted like weapons. The entire room seemed to lean in, breath held, waiting for the explosion.

Alex looked up slowly, his expression unchanged, but he didn't speak.

Beth's voice cracked the silence like a whip, "You gonna keep pretending I don't exist, or are we doing this now?"

He met her eyes, and still said nothing.

She leaned in, knuckles white on the table. "I've spent the last three days getting shredded in every group chat, every hallway, every fucking bathroom. And you—" Her laugh was bitter, jagged. "—you've sent me three texts. Three. No calls. No, 'I've got your back.' Nothing. You let Patty spin this however she wants, and you just... sit here. Eating a burger like it's not happening."

Still nothing from him. He picked up a fry, twirled it between his fingers, then dropped it back on the tray.

Jake shifted uncomfortably. "Beth, maybe—"

"Shut up, Jake," she snapped without looking at him. Her eyes stayed locked on Alex. "I'm talking to the guy who fucked me senseless Friday night, and then ghosted me the second the consequences showed up. If you think I can't handle the rumors, then fine, but you don't get to act like I'm invisible while everyone else tears me apart."

The silence stretched, thick and electric. Someone in the back coughed. A phone camera clicked.

Alex finally spoke. Low, and calm, too calm, his only statement, "You done?"

Beth blinked. "Excuse me?"

"You done yelling?" He leaned back in his chair, arms crossing over his chest. "Because, if you're looking for me to make a big public apology or start swinging at everyone who's talking shit, that's not happening."

Her mouth opened, then closed. Heat climbed up her neck.

"So that's it? You're just gonna sit there and let them say whatever they want about me? About us?"

"Us? I'm not letting them do anything, but I'm not the one playing into the drama circus. Patty wants a spectacle, and look around, you're giving her one right now."

Beth laughed again—short, incredulous. "You, you're unbelievable. I'm the one getting dragged through the mud, and you're worried about optics, incredible."

"We hooked up at a party, new girl, there's no 'us.'"

The words landed like a slap. She straightened, hands sliding off the table, fingers curling into fists at her sides.

Alex exhaled through his nose. He looked away for the first time since she slammed the table. His jaw ticked once.

Beth waited. The cafeteria waited. No one breathed.

When he looked back, his eyes were tired. Not angry. Just... tired.

Her voice dropped to something cold and precise. "I see, you didn't think I would show up to call you on your bullshit."

"What bullshit? I've been trying to keep this from turning into a bigger shit-show, but if that's what you want, then have at it."

Beth stared at him until the anger settled. She stepped back from the table. The circle of onlookers parted slightly, like they sensed the fuse had been pulled.

Alex held her gaze for a long beat, then he pushed his chair back and stood up, slowly and deliberately.

The cafeteria exhaled as one.

"Here it all is, Beth, all the drama, in all its glory. Is this what you wanted?"

She chuckled. "Just forget about me, Alex, like I never existed!

"Fine!" he barked.

She said no more, looked up at him with a fluttering hidden sadness, then straitened her composure again with a glance out at the sea of faces still watching them, then she turned away and walked out.

The cafeteria erupted into noise the second she was gone.

Chapter 14

The Social Pyramid

The afternoon sun slanted low through the high windows of the auxiliary gym, turning the blue mats gold and casting long shadows across the squad. The music was already thumping—some aggressive pop remix with a heavy drop—and the girls were mid-stunt: bases locked, flyers climbing, the pyramid rising clean and sharp before collapsing into a controlled tumble. Sweat glistened on bare midriffs; ponytails whipped like flags.

Beth stood just inside the double doors, backpack slung over one shoulder, still in her jeans and hoodie from the day. She hadn't changed into anything athletic yet. She hadn't even brought proper shoes. She just... showed up.

Samantha, the captain, spotted her first, but she didn't stop leading the squad. She stayed at the front, calling counts in that clipped, no-bullshit tone she used when she was in full command mode. She didn't miss a beat—eyes flicked to Beth, held for half a second, then she barked, "Hold! Reset! Water if you need it—thirty seconds."

The formation broke. Girls dropped to mats, grabbed bottles, wiped faces with the hems of their tanks. A few glanced Beth's way—curious, wary, sizing up the new rumor magnet who'd just walked into their territory.

Samantha strode over, barefoot on the mat, arms crossed, a faint sheen of sweat on her collarbones. She stopped a foot away and looked Beth up and down like she was inspecting equipment.

"You're late," Samantha said.

Beth checked her phone half-heartedly, and then shrugged.

Samantha's mouth twitched. "Smartass." She jerked her head toward the side wall where a stack of spare uniforms sat folded on a bench. "Grab one, shorts, top, hair up. You're trying out right now."

Beth raised an eyebrow. "I thought you said I was in if I showed?"

"You are, but you still have to be—" she stroked her hair in thought, "—initiated."

A couple of the girls nearby exchanged looks—half amused, half impressed. One whispered something to her neighbor; the other nodded like this was classic Samantha.

Beth didn't argue. She dropped her backpack, walked to the bench, and picked up the top piece: crimson cropped tank with gold lettering across the chest—**SQUAD** in bold block letters. The shorts were matching, tiny, high-cut. She glanced at the tag—size small. It would fit. Barely.

She kicked off her sneakers, peeled the hoodie over her head (revealing the plain black sports bra she'd worn under it), then shimmied out of her jeans. The gym went quieter for a second—eyes flicking her way, then politely away again. She stepped into the shorts, tugged the tank down, and adjusted the straps. Hair came out of the messy bun, got twisted into a high, tight ponytail in three quick moves. No mirror needed; she'd done this enough times growing up.

When she turned back, Samantha was waiting, arms still crossed, but now with a small, approving smirk.

"Not bad," she said. "You look like you belong. Let's see if you move like it."

Beth followed her to the center of the mat. The squad had reformed loosely around them—bases in position, flyers stretching, everyone watching without pretending otherwise.

Samantha clapped once. "Basic eight-count. Arms sharp, feet pointed, smile like you mean it. Follow me."

She demonstrated—clean, precise, every movement hitting the beat like it owed her money. Beth mirrored it. First rep was stiff, muscle memory rusty. Second was better. Third, her shoulders dropped, hips loosened, and the motion started to feel natural.

Samantha didn't comment, just nodded once and moved to the next sequence—high V, low V, T-motion, touchdown, then a quick pivot into a heel stretch prep. Beth kept up, even when Samantha threw in a surprise clap-stomp-clap that caught half the squad off-guard.

After ten minutes of nonstop basics, Samantha called a halt.

"Pyramid time," she announced to the group. "Beth—you're going flyer. Middle layer, right side. Don't drop."

Beth's stomach flipped. She nodded, stepped into position.

The bases locked arms. Beth planted one foot in the cradle of two sets of hands, gripped shoulders for balance, and pushed off. Strong. Steady. The pyramid rose—three tiers, clean lines, no wobble. She hit the top pose: arms in a high V, leg extended in a liberty, chin up, smile forced but convincing.

The hold lasted five seconds. Then Samantha barked, "Dismount!"

They brought her down controlled, feet hitting the mat softly.

Silence for a beat.

Then Samantha nodded—once, sharply.

"You're in," she said. No ceremony, no applause. Just a fact.

A ripple of murmurs went through the squad. A few girls grinned. One—tall, dark ponytail, probably a senior base—gave Beth a quick fist bump as she walked past.

Beth exhaled, adrenaline still buzzing under her skin.

Samantha stepped close, voice low so only Beth could hear.

"Patty's gonna lose her mind when she sees you in uniform at the next game. That's the point. You're not just on the squad—you're the reminder she doesn't own this place anymore." She paused. "And if anyone gives you shit, you tell me. I handle my girls."

Beth met her eyes. "Got it."

Samantha smirked again. "Good. Now grab a water and get back in line. We're running the full routine from the top. Welcome to the squad, troublemaker."

Beth grabbed a bottle from the cooler, twisted the cap, and took a long drink.

The music kicked back on.

She stepped into formation.

For the first time in days, the knot in her chest felt less like a noose and more like fuel.

She was going to burn bright.

And she was going to make sure everyone saw.

Chapter 15

A Strange Alliance

Beth noticed the shift on Wednesday afternoon, subtle as a tide pulling back.

The cafeteria had stopped hushing when she walked in. Whispers still followed, but they were softer now—background noise instead of gunfire. The sideways glances had lost their edge; some even turned into quick, awkward nods. The rumor-mill hadn't died, but it was cooling, running low on fresh fuel. People were bored, and she thought they were deserving of a new show.

She hated that feeling more than the hate itself, being irrelevant again. She quickly felt as if she might be fading back into social wallpaper with a 'transfer-girl' label.

She walked the halls slower than usual, eyes scanning all faces she hadn't bothered memorizing before. Now she was hunting again. Freshmen mostly—wide-eyed, still oblivious to the social hierarchy just as much more that they were trying to find their own place to belong. A few sophomores who kept to their own clusters. The occasional senior who'd somehow missed the entire drama (impressive, considering how loud it had been). She smiled at strangers, held eye contact a beat too long, dropped casual hellos in passing. Testing. Cataloging. Looking for anyone who didn't flinch when they heard her name, anyone who hadn't already decided what she was.

Most reacted the same: flicker of recognition, tion, quick retreat, or forced politeness. She filed them away—too easy, too predictable. She needed someone new. Someone clean.

She was almost ready to give up for the day—backpack slung over one shoulder, heading toward the parking lot—when a voice called her name from behind.

"Beth? Hey—wait up."

She turned.

The girl jogging toward her was small, compact, with lush, wavy brown hair. She wore a distinctly 'normal-girl' outfit, a simple top, typical jeans, and scuffed Converse. No makeup. No pretense. Just... there.

"I'm Lainey," she said, stopping a respectful distance away, slightly out of breath. "I've seen you around. Thought maybe... we could talk?"

Beth tilted her head. "About?"

Lainey shrugged, hands shoved deep in her pockets. "Nothing big. Just... you seem interesting, and, maybe in need of a friend."

Beth studied her. No smirk. No knowing glint. No immediate mention of the rumors. Just earnest, almost painfully straightforward.

She decided to test it.

"You know who I am, right?" Beth asked, voice flat.

Lainey nodded once. "Yeah. I know the rumors. Everyone does." She didn't flinch, didn't look away. "Doesn't mean I believe the version that's going around. Or that I think you're some villain who needs to be shunned."

Beth's brows lifted slightly. "Most people do."

"Most people are lazy," Lainey said simply. "They hear one story and stop asking questions. I don't." She shifted her weight, looking almost shy for the first time. "I think everyone should get their side heard. Even if it's messy. Even if they're trying to make a name for themselves at a school that chews people up for fun. Doesn't make you evil. Just... human."

Beth felt something twist in her chest—surprise, maybe suspicion. Lainey wasn't performing.

She wasn't fishing for gossip or trying to get close for clout. She was just... sincere. Painfully sincere.

And that made her perfect.

Beth smiled—slow, small, the kind she saved for when she was already three steps ahead.

"You're kind of a nobody here, aren't you?" she asked, not unkindly.

Lainey laughed, short and self-aware. "Pretty much. I've had the same few friends for years. We keep our heads down. No sports, no parties, no drama. Just... existing."

Beth nodded. "I like that."

Beth's thoughts coiled with raw malevolence and excitement: a new, pristine, untouched canvas waiting for her to splash her will across it. This girl actually believed she could fix her—save the girl who happily torched half the school just because she felt like it. And she planned to step right into her line of fire without asking for anything in return. How delightedly reckless.

Lainey's eyes had that quiet, hopeful light—the one that said she believed everyone deserved second chances. That underneath Beth's calculated chaos and the sharp edges, there was someone worth redeeming.

Beth hated that light. It made her want to snuff it out just to see what happened.

But she also liked it. Liked the challenge. Liked the idea of letting Lainey get close—close enough to trust her, close enough to care—before she twisted the knife.

"So," Beth said, shifting her backpack. "You want to be friends?"

Lainey's face brightened. "Yeah. I do."

Chapter 16

The Day I Met The Devil

Beth decided to play the long game with Lainey.

She kept her voice softer around her, her smiles smaller, her edges tucked in. No more hallway confrontations. No more dropping bombs in the cafeteria. She let the rumor mill keep cooling on its own while she walked beside Lainey between classes, laughed at her dry jokes, and asked about her favorite bands, all to act like she actually cared. She wanted Lainey to think she was retreating—licking her wounds, finally ready to fade into the background, grateful for a quiet friend who didn't judge.

It was the perfect cover.

They were sitting on the low stone wall outside the arts building during free period, sharing a bag of sour gummy worms Lainey had pulled from her backpack. Beth was mid-sentence—something deliberately banal about hating early-morning math—when a guy rounded the corner and spotted them.

He was young-looking. His curly dark hair jumped in and out of his eyes as he walked in a careless way that looked intentional. Black hoodie, faded jeans. He had the same sharp cheekbones as Lainey, the same wary intelligence in his gaze.

"Lane," he said, voice low and amused. "You didn't tell me you were collecting strays now."

Lainey rolled her eyes but smiled. "Benny. Go away. We're bonding."

Ben—Benny—didn't move. His eyes slid to Beth, slow and unhurried, like he was reading fine print. Recognition flickered there, quick and bright. He knew exactly who she was.

Beth met his stare head-on, chin tilted just enough. "Hi," she said sweetly. "You must be the brother."

"Ben," he corrected, ignoring the nickname. "And yeah. I've heard about you."

Lainey stood up fast, brushing crumbs off her jeans. "Ben. Walk with me. Now."

She grabbed his sleeve and tugged him ten feet away, toward the shade of a big oak. Beth stayed put, popping another gummy worm in her mouth, pretending not to watch.

Lainey's voice was low but sharp enough to carry fragments.

"...stay out of her orbit, seriously. She's not... she's no good for you. You're young, you don't need that kind of mess in your life."

Ben's laugh was quiet, almost fond. "I know who she is, Lane. That's why I'm interested."

Lainey hissed something Beth couldn't catch, but the exasperation was clear. Ben just shrugged, hands in his pockets, looking back over Lainey's shoulder straight at Beth again. He didn't smile. Didn't look away.

Lainey threw her hands up, muttered something that sounded like 'You're impossible,' then stomped back toward the wall.

She stopped in front of Beth, arms crossed.

"Don't," she said flatly.

Beth blinked with innocence. "Don't what?"

"Don't play with him, he's my brother. He's... he likes trouble. And you're currently the walking definition of it."

Beth tilted her head. "I'm just trying to lay low, Lay-Lay. You said it yourself—everyone deserves a chance to fix their mistakes. I'm not looking for more drama."

Lainey studied her for a long beat, eyes narrowed, "Yeah. Sure." She exhaled hard. "Just... don't blame me if I can't trust you just yet, either of you."

She shot one last warning look at Ben—still standing by the tree—then turned and headed toward her next class without another word.

Beth waited until Lainey was out of earshot.

Then she stood, slung her backpack over one shoulder, and walked straight toward Ben.

He didn't move as she approached. He just watched her, expression unreadable.

"Protective sister," Beth observed.

"She's smart," he said. "She knows you're dangerous."

Beth stopped a few feet away, far enough that he'd have to change his gaze to meet her eyes. "And you like that, Benjamin."

Ben's mouth curved—just the corner. "Yeah," he said, "something like that."

She let the silence stretch, let him feel the weight of her stare. Then she shrugged, light and careless. "I'm just trying to be good. You know: lay low, make friends, be boring."

He snorted softly. "Aha, 'boring' says the gossipee, interesting because you're no good at boring, Beth."

Beth smiled—small, real for once. "Maybe," she winked, "but I'm very good at interesting."

Ben studied her for another second, then pulled his phone out of his pocket. "Give me your number."

She raised a brow. "Bossy."

"Curious," he corrected.

She rattled off the digits. He typed them in, thumb rushing to keep up.

"Done," he said, pocketing his phone again. "I'll text you later. See if you're still pretending to be harmless."

Beth laughed under her breath. "You won't be disappointed."

He gave her one last long look—assessing, intrigued, a little reckless—then turned and walked off toward the parking lot.

Beth watched him go, heart beating a little faster than it should have.

The rest of the day dragged—classes, hallways, the usual low simmer of eyes on her—but her mind kept circling back to that look in his eyes. Dangerous. Interested. Unafraid.

By the time the final bell rang, her phone buzzed. Unknown number:

Still laying low? Or ready to stop pretending? —Ben

She stared at the screen for a beat.

She saved his number and ignored the text.

She smiled to herself, slow and sharp.

Lainey could try to keep them apart all she wanted.

Beth was already in orbit.

And Ben was already falling.

Chapter 17

Saturday Night Haze

The cheer squad's Saturday night ritual was sacred: no parents, no boyfriends, phones on silent. Sam's giant family estate was a perfect place for the meetup; she had her own wing in the house. Fairy lights strung across her own living room, a playlist that shifted from throwback pop to whatever viral sound was inescapable that week, and enough spiked seltzer to keep everyone loose but not sloppy.

Tonight, the energy was different. Electric. The girls kept glancing at the front door every time headlights swept across the windows.

"Where the hell is she?" Jenna muttered, swirling her drink. "She better not flake."

Samantha, perched on the arm of the couch like a queen on her throne, smirked. "She won't. Beth's too invested now. She knows what's at stake."

The doorbell rang—sharp, confident.

Kayla bolted over to open it.

Beth stepped inside wearing her cheer uniform covered by an oversized cropped hoodie (squad colors still, red and gold), and white sneakers. Hair in a high pony, minimal makeup, looking like she'd just rolled out of bed before practice. She scanned the room once—quick, assessing—then smiled the small, easy smile she'd been perfecting around them.

"Hey, squad," she said, casual as anything.

A chorus of cheers and whoops went up. Someone handed her a drink before she even set her bag down. Other girls' arms slung around her shoulders, and compliments flew high—hair, outfit, the way she'd landed that last stunt at practice. She fit in like she'd been there for years.

Samantha waited until the initial wave passed, then crooked a finger. Beth followed her into the kitchen, away from the main noise.

"You've been quiet," Sam said, leaning against the counter, arms crossed. "Too quiet. We had an agreement. You were supposed to keep the rumor pot bubbling. Stir shit. Give Patty something fresh to choke on. Instead, you're playing nice-girl transfer who just wants friends. What gives?"

Beth took a slow sip of her drink, eyes never leaving Sam's. She set the cup down with a soft clink, lips curving into a lazy, unapologetic smirk.

"Oops. My bad," she drawled, voice dripping with mock innocence. "Didn't realize I was on a schedule to be your personal chaos agent. Guess I got distracted by all the... extracurriculars."

Sam's mouth twitched, fighting a grin. "Please, bitch, call me Sam."

Before Beth could fire back, Jenna's voice cut in from the living room, loud enough to carry over the music.

"Beth! Why the hell are you in uniform? You look like you're about to run drills at 6 p.m. on a Saturday."

Laughter rippled through the room. Riley leaned over the back of the couch, eyeing Beth's cropped crimson tank and tiny shorts peaking from under her cheer skirt. "Seriously. Did you think we were practicing tonight? Like, actual cheer practice? On a weekend? Shame"

Beth glanced down at herself, then shrugged, spinning once so the high ponytail whipped dramatically. "I look cute. You're all basically wearing pajamas that double as lingerie. Uniform's basically the same thing."

Kayla snorted. "Uniform's cute on you, newbie, but you're giving 'eager freshman' vibes. Strip down like the rest of us, you're off the clock."

Beth rolled her eyes, but she was grinning. "Fine, fine. I'll change when I feel like it. Until then, enjoy the view."

She turned back to Sam, lowering her voice just enough. "Anyway, like I was saying—I'm working on something bigger. Trust me. It needs time to build. Rushing it would make it look desperate. I don't do desperate."

Sam studied her for a beat, arms still crossed, but the edge had softened. "It better be good."

Beth leaned in, close, whispering over the counter, "It's going to be legendary."

Sam studied her for a long beat. "You better not be going soft on me, troublemaker."

Before Beth could answer, Jenna burst into the kitchen, eyes bright, cheeks already flushed from whatever was in her cup.

"Sam. Beth. It's time." Jenna's grin was wicked. "Beth has to do, you know... the thing."

Sam's expression shifted—annoyance melting into anticipation. "Oh yes, yes she does."

Beth raised a brow. "Care to fill me in?"

Jenna bounced on her toes. "Hazing tradition. The new girl has to pull off a classic.

The room went quiet for half a second.

Beth set her drink down. "What do you want me to do? Eat something gross, streak through the quad?"

Jenna clapped slowly. "She's perfect."

Sam pushed off the counter. "Let's move."

The squad piled into Sam's SUV—music blasting, windows down, laughter spilling into the night.

"So what am I doing anyway?"

You're stealing all of Patty's underwear. Every single pair."

We roll up, lights off, you find a way in, stuff them thangs in the bag, out in under two minutes. Easy, right?"

Beth shrugged. "Piece of cake."

They parked one street over from Patty's place, killed the engines, and crept the rest of the way on foot.

The house loomed darker than Beth remembered, a two-story brick colonial with black shutters that swallowed the moonlight. No porch light. No motion-sensor flood. Just the faint blue glow of a TV left on somewhere downstairs, flickering through half-closed blinds like a dying heartbeat. The night air was cool and still, carrying the distant bark of a neighbor's dog and the low hum of traffic two streets over.

Beth crouched low behind a row of trimmed boxwoods that lined the side yard, drawstring bag slung tight against her spine. Her squad hoodie was zipped to her chin, hood up, sleeves pulled over her hands. She breathed slowly through her nose—steady, controlled—watching the windows for any shift in light, any shadow that didn't belong.

She knew Patty was none the wiser to her presence, yet she still felt exposed, creeping around the dark grounds of the property, knowing she didn't belong there, like some spy in the movies. She edged around the corner of the garage, but she couldn't go that way. Bright white lightbulbs waited there to betray her the second she crossed the threshold.

The front door was out. Too exposed. The back slider would probably be locked, too. Her parents were always gone, right? Yeah, but they wouldn't leave the house vulnerable.

She cursed under her breath, retreating into the shadow of the garage. Options narrowed fast.

Side gate—locked, chain rattling when she tested it. Front porch—no cover. Windows on the ground floor—all latched tight, curtains drawn. She circled back to the far side of the house, staying close to the brick, footsteps silent on the mulch.

That's when she saw it.

Upstairs, second-floor window on the left side—guest room. The same one she and Alex had shared while Patty slept down the hall. It was cracked open maybe two inches, just enough for a breeze to stir the sheer curtain inside. A thin ribbon of moonlight slipped through the gap, catching on the white frame.

Perfect.

Except, it was upstairs.

No ladder. No trellis. Just smooth brick and a narrow decorative ledge that ran below the second-story windows—maybe eight inches wide, barely enough for toes.

Beth tilted her head back, measuring the height. Ten, twelve feet to the ledge. Doable... if she could reach it.

She scanned the yard again—nothing useful. Then her eyes landed on the downspout running down the corner of the house, ten feet to her right. Aluminum, painted black to match the shutters, bolted every few feet. Sturdy enough, probably.

She moved quickly and quietly, pressing her back to the wall beside the spout. Gripped it with both hands—cold metal biting into her palms—and tested her weight. It held. She planted one sneaker against the brick, found a foothold on the first bracket, and pulled herself up.

The climb was slow, deliberate. Hand over hand, toes scraping for purchase on the narrow brackets. Halfway up, the spout gave a soft metallic groan. She froze, heart slamming against her ribs, waiting for lights, for shouts, for anything.

Nothing came. Just the wind rustling the leaves overhead.

She kept going.

At the top, the ledge was right there—eye level now. She hooked one arm over it, biceps burning, then swung her leg up and hooked her knee. The brick was rough against her thigh as she hauled herself onto the narrow shelf, balancing on the balls of her feet, back pressed flat to the wall. The drop below looked farther than it had from the ground.

She edged sideways—slow and careful—each step, sliding her sneaker along the ledge, fingers splayed against the brick for balance. Four feet. Six. Eight. Then came the guest-room window.

She reached out, fingertips brushing the sash. Pushed gently.

It gave.

The window slid up another four inches with only the faintest squeak of old paint. Beth exhaled through her teeth, then gripped the frame with both hands and squeezed herself through—head first, shoulders twisting, hips scraping the sill. She tumbled inside in a controlled roll, landing on the hard floor with a soft thud.

The room smelled faintly of laundry detergent and Alex's cologne—still lingering on the pillows, probably. Moonlight slanted across the bed, illuminating the same rumpled sheets they'd wrecked not so long ago. For half a second, memory hit her like a sharp knife: his hands on her hips, her name in his mouth, the mirror across the room reflecting every filthy second.

She shoved it down.

No time.

She rose to a crouch, listening. The house was quiet—only the low tick of a clock somewhere downstairs, the faint hum of the fridge. Patty's room was at the other end of the hall. No footsteps. No lights.

Beth crept to the door and cracked it open inch by inch.

Hallway dark. Empty.

She waited for what seemed like an eternity.

Then it happened. Footsteps. Then a shadow. More footsteps…

Patty was going down the stairs. She listened for a moment more. A light switch.

That's it—now or never.

She slipped out of the doorway, trickling toward Patty's room like a shadow.

Patty's room smelled like vanilla candle and expensive perfume. Beth had to admit, there was probably more stench than light in there, but she had to work with the little light she had. She went straight for the dresser—top drawer, lacy thongs and boyshorts in every color. She swept them into the black drawstring bag she'd brought, fast and efficient. Done.

She was halfway turned around when the light snapped on.

Patty stood there in oversized sweats and a messy bun, phone already in hand, eyes wide, then narrowing into slits.

"What the actual fuck?"

Beth froze for half a heartbeat—then bolted past her.

Patty screamed—a full-throated, furious wail—and gave chase.

Beth sprinted down the stairs and through the living room, bag swinging, sneakers spanking tile. Patty was right behind her, yelling incoherently: "You psycho! Give that back! I'm calling the cops!"

Beth yanked open the front door and burst out into the free world.

The squad was already scattering—some sprinting toward the street, others diving behind bushes.

Patty made it to the porch, phone to her ear, voice shrill: "Yes, police? There's someone in my house—stealing my underwear! Yes, right now!"

Beth didn't stop running until she reached the SUV. The girls piled in, doors slamming, engines roaring to life. Tires squealed as they peeled out.

Breathless laughter exploded.

"Did you get them all?" Jenna demanded.

Beth held up the bulging bag like a trophy. "Every last one."

Sam, behind the wheel, cackled. "Holy shit. She actually called the cops."

Beth leaned back against the seat, adrenaline singing through her veins, grin wide and reckless.

"Let her call. Let them come. We're gone."

She glanced out the window at the receding streetlights, the bag of stolen underwear on the dashboard like stolen evidence.

The rumor pot wasn't just bubbling anymore.

It was boiling over.

And Beth was the one turning up the heat.

Chapter 18

Girls Like Trouble

The SUV rolled back into the long, winding driveway of Samantha's estate just after midnight, the engine cut off, leaving a deafening silence. The whole thing felt like the end of a heist movie. The girls spilled out laughing before the doors even fully opened—high-pitched, breathless giggles that echoed off the quiet suburban street.

They cleanly swept through the giant entrance way, quickly toeing deep into the east wing that was still a mess from earlier. Inside, the sitting room, one of the sitting rooms, was still warm and softly lit, contrasted by an aura of snarky chatter and the spirit of hollow mean girl tension. Someone cranked the playlist back up—low enough not to draw in Sam's parents, loud enough to keep them out. Bags of chips got ripped open, and drinks got refreshed. Beth tossed the black drawstring bag of Patty's stolen underwear landed in the center of the coffee table like a trophy.

Jenna flopped onto the couch first, kicking her feet up. "Okay, but when she screamed 'Give that back!'—I swear I felt it in my soul."

Sarah mimicked Patty's voice, high and furious: "'There's someone in my house—stealing my underwear!' Like, girl, own it! You called the cops over panties!"

The room dissolved into fresh laughter. Beth dropped onto the arm of the sectional next to Sam, legs crossed, still buzzing from the stunt.

Samantha leaned forward, grabbed the bag, and upended it. A rainbow of lace and cotton tumbled out—thongs, boyshorts, a few surprisingly plain panties.

Beth held up a pair of high-waisted, floral cotton briefs with a dramatic flourish. "Behold, the queen's secret weapon!"

Jenna snatched them, dangling them from one finger. "These? These are straight-up granny panties with extra steps. I bet she irons them."

Beth joined in, "No wonder she's so uptight. Those things are basically chastity belts."

Debra pointed at Beth, eyes sparkling. "Wait, wait—don't act like you're above it, new girl. I bet that's what you wear under the uniform. Full coverage spread, practical and boring."

Beth arched a brow, a slow smile spreading. "You wanna bet?"

The room went quiet for half a second—then erupted.

"Prove it!" Jenna chanted, clapping her hands. "Prove it! Prove it!"

Samantha leaned back, arms crossed, grin wicked. "Yeah, troublemaker, show us what you're working with."

Beth stood up without hesitation, in the middle of the circle, the squad forming a loose ring around her like they were performing a ritual. She hooked her thumbs under the spandex rim of her athletic shorts and peeled them down slowly, deliberately, teasing—revealing the smooth skin of her lower abdomen. She clinched her shorts one last time and dropped them to the floor. The shorts fell quickly, slid down her thighs, pooling at her ankles. She stepped out of them in one smooth motion, flinging them from her foot. Underneath: simple black cheeky panties—high-cut, lace-trimmed, sexy without trying too hard, nothing granny about them.

The girls whooped.

"Called it!" Debra crowed.

Beth spun once, arms out, owning it. "Told you."

Samantha's eyes lingered a beat longer than the rest. She tilted her head, voice dropping low and half-joking. "Okay, but mine are cuter."

Beth turned to her, challenge in her smile. "Prove it."

The room went dead silent again—then exploded.

Samantha laughed—sharp, surprised—and pushed off the couch. "Fine. But only because I know I win."

She hooked her thumbs into the waistband of her gray sweatpants, shoved them down, and kicked them off. Underneath: bright red bikini-cut panties with thin side ties and a tiny bow.

The squad lost it—screaming, laughing, someone yelling "Get a room!" while another started a slow clap.

Jenna leaned forward, grinning like a Cheshire cat. "Okay, okay—bet you two won't kiss though."

Debra jumped in. "All talk, no follow-through, that's not like you, Sammy."

Sam barked back, "Shut up, D.D."

Beth glanced at Samantha. Sam's eyes were bright, pupils blown from the adrenaline and the alcohol and maybe something else. She shrugged one shoulder—casual, daring.

"Your call, troublemaker."

Beth stepped closer—slow, deliberate—until they were inches apart. The room held its breath.

She reached up, tucked a loose strand of hair behind Samantha's ear, then leaned in and brushed her lips against Sam's—just a tease, just enough to make it count. Soft. Quick. Electric.

When she pulled back, Samantha's cheeks were flushed, her grin crooked, slightly dangerous.

The squad detonated—screams, whistles, someone throwing a pillow.

Beth laughed, stepping back, hands up. "Happy now?"

Jenna fanned herself. "Jesus. I need a cold shower."

Samantha picked up her sweatpants, still smirking. "Told you mine are cuter."

Beth dropped back onto the couch, legs stretched out, completely at ease. "Yeah, well… next time bring better competition."

The night rolled on, but the energy had shifted. The hazing was done, and Beth wasn't just in the squad anymore; she was one of them.

Chapter 19
I Kissed a Girl

Sam turned down the music a little as she sensed that night was starting to get late, but it only made the air feel thicker as time suddenly became more apparent. Most of the squad had scattered a bit throughout the night; some went home, others sprawled on the floor with blankets, some shared guest beds, and the rest of them, groggy, barely awake. The main room's lights were dimmed to just the string lights and a single lamp in the corner, casting everything in warm amber.

Beth and Sam were still on the sectional, thighs pressed together, the space between them electric. The kiss earlier had been a dare, a performance for the crowd. This felt different—quieter, heavier, inevitable.

Sam's hand rested high on Beth's thigh, thumb tracing slow, absent circles over bare skin. Beth's fingers played with the thin red strap of Sam's bikini panties, tugging lightly, letting it snap back against her hipbone.

"You're staring," Sam murmured, voice rough from laughing and drinking and whatever else was building between them.

Beth leaned in, lips brushing the shell of Sam's ear. "I'm still picturing you naked."

Sam's breath hitched. She turned her head, caught Beth's mouth in a kiss that started slow—testing, teasing—then deepened fast. Tongues sliding, teeth grazing lower lip, hands moving with purpose now. Sam's palm slid up Beth's side, under the sports bra, cupping the weight of her breast, thumb brushing over a nipple that was already tight and sensitive.

Beth moaned softly into the kiss—quiet enough that it stayed between them, but loud enough that Jenna, sprawled on the rug nearby, glanced over and smirked before pointedly looking away.

They broke apart just long enough for Sam to stand, tugging Beth up with her. No words. Just fingers laced, a quick glance around to make sure the room was distracted enough, then they headed down the hallway toward Sam's bedroom.

The door clicked shut.

The room was small—a queen bed, fairy lights looped around the headboard, a half-open closet spilling hoodies and cheer bags. Moonlight sliced through the blinds in thin silver bars.

Sam pushed Beth back against the door, bodies flush, mouths crashing again. Hands everywhere—Sam's shoving Beth's sports bra up and off, Beth's yanking Sam's tank over her head, red panties tugged down just enough to bare her. Skin on skin, heat building fast.

Beth's back hit the mattress first. Sam followed, straddling her hips, grinding down with a longing lust. Beth arched up, hands gripping Sam's ass, pulling her closer, harder. Their mouths met again—messy, open, wet. Sam's fingers found Beth's nipple, pinched, rolled, and tugged until Beth gasped into her mouth.

"Fuck," Beth breathed. "You're good at that."

Sam grinned against her throat, teeth scraping skin.

She slid lower—kissing down Beth's sternum, between her breasts, tongue circling one nipple while fingers teased the other. Beth's hips rolled up, seeking friction. Sam obliged—sliding a hand between Beth's thighs, pushing the black cheeky panties aside, fingers gliding across her hot, pulsing labia.

Beth's head fell back. "God—yes."

Sam didn't tease long. Two fingers slid inside, slow and precise—deep, curling. Beth's thighs trembled, hands fisting the sheets. Sam worked her steadily—faster, then slower, then faster again—watching Beth's face the whole time, cataloging every look of pleasure, and every moan.

Beth came hard—harder than she expected—her whole body seizing in a violent, shuddering wave. Her inner walls clamped down around Sam's fingers like a vise, pulsing in frantic, rhythmic contractions. Sam kept going, fingers curling relentlessly against that swollen spot inside, her thumb giving a sensible deride of attention to her clit, refusing to let the peak crest and fade.

Then it happened.

A sudden, overwhelming pressure built low in Beth's belly—sharp, almost painful in its intensity. She gasped, tried to warn Sam, but the words dissolved into a broken whimper. Her hips jerked up involuntarily, thighs trembling uncontrollably, and then she shattered...

A hot, clear gush erupted from her—forceful, uncontrollable—splashing across Sam's wrist, forearm, chest, and higher still. It arced in a glistening spray, catching Sam square across the cheek and lips, dripping down her chin in slow, obscene rivulets. More followed, soaking the sheets beneath them in a wide, dark wet spot that spread fast, warm, and slick. Beth's body kept spasming, each pulse sending another smaller jet, until the last one trickled down her own thighs.

She collapsed back, chest heaving, eyes wide with shock and mortification. Her face burned crimson.

"Oh my god—Sam—I'm so sorry—" The words tumbled out in a garbled rush, voice cracking with embarrassment. "I've never—I didn't even know I could—I'm so fucking sorry, that's so gross, I—"

Sam lifted her head slowly, deliberately. Her lips glistened, cheeks streaked, dark hair clinging damply to her forehead. She licked her bottom lip once—slow, savoring—then crawled up Beth's body until their faces were inches apart.

"Shut up," Sam said, voice low and wrecked, eyes blazing with something hungry and reverent. "Don't you dare apologize for that."

Beth blinked, still flush and trembling. "But I just—your face, the bed—"

Sam cut her off with a kiss—deep, filthy, tasting of Beth herself. She pressed their bodies together, slick skin sliding against slick skin, the wet spot between them cool now but still warm from their heat.

"That was the hottest fucking thing I've ever seen," Sam murmured against her mouth. "You soaked me. You soaked everything. And you're still shaking like you want more."

Beth let out a shaky laugh, half sob, half relief. "I thought I broke something."

"You didn't break anything." Sam's fingers traced the line of Beth's jaw, thumb brushing over her swollen lower lip. "You just came so hard you squirted all over me," she drew a slow kiss from her, "and I loved every second of it."

Beth searched her face—looking for disgust, for teasing, for anything but the raw want she found there.

Sam kissed her again, softer this time. "No shame. No sorry. Just... fuck, do that again."

Beth exhaled a trembling breath, the embarrassment melting into something warm and bolder. She hooked a leg around Sam's waist, pulling her closer, feeling the fresh slickness between them.

"You're insane," she whispered.

Sam grinned as she arched above her with a wicked glow. "Look at you, still dripping."

Beth's laugh dissolved into a moan as Sam's hand slid back between her thighs, fingers gliding through the mess they'd made, already coaxing her sensitive nerves back to life.

"Your turn," Beth rasped, flipping them so fast Sam barely had time to react.

Now Beth was on top—mouth on Sam's neck, then lower, kissing the red bow on her panties before tugging them off with her teeth. Sam laughed—low, wrecked—blissfully helpless to the feel of Beth slowly crawling down her. Kiss after kiss, Beth gained charge over her. Sam too lit with contractions of silent shrill like an electric tine screaming into a void. She let out the most approving involuntary moan when Beth's tongue found her clit, flat and slow at first, then flicking, sucking, relentless.

Sam's hands tangled in Beth's hair, hips rocking up to meet every stroke. Beth slid two fingers inside, curled them, pumped in time with her tongue. Sam's thighs clamped around her head, breath coming in sharp pants.

"Fuck—Beth—right there—"

Sam shattered with a low, guttural groan, body bowing, fingers tightening in Beth's hair until it hurt in the best way. Beth worked her through it—gentler now, softer licks, easing her down.

They collapsed together—sweaty, breathless, tangled limbs. Sam's head on Beth's chest, Beth's fingers tracing lazy patterns on Sam's back.

After a long minute, Sam lifted her head, a smirk returning. "We're not done."

Beth's laugh was low, wrecked, still catching her breath. "You're gonna kill me."

Sam's eyes darkened, pupils blown wide in the dim light. "Not yet."

She shifted, slow and predatory, sliding up Beth's body until her knees bracketed Beth's head. The mattress dipped under her weight. Beth looked up—Sam towering above her, thighs strong and slick, skin flushed from earlier orgasms, hair falling forward like a dark curtain. Sam reached down, fingers threading roughly through Beth's hair, tugging just enough to tilt her chin up.

"Open," Sam ordered, voice thick, commanding.

Beth obeyed without hesitation—mouth parting, tongue already flat and waiting.

Sam lowered herself slowly—agonizingly slow—until her wet heat settled over Beth's mouth. She didn't drop her full weight at first; she hovered, teasing, letting Beth feel the heat radiating off her, the slick glide of arousal already coating her lips. Beth's hands came up instinctively, gripping Sam's thighs, thumbs digging into the soft flesh just below the curve of her ass.

Then Sam sank down.

Beth moaned into her vibration, humming straight through Sam's clit. Sam's hips rolled once, experimental, testing. Beth's tongue met her eagerly—long, flat strokes from entrance to clit, then flicking tight circles at the swollen bud. Sam's breath hitched, fingers tightening in Beth's hair until it stung.

"Good girl," Sam rasped, starting to grind in earnest now—slow, filthy circles, dragging herself over Beth's tongue, her nose, her chin. The wet sounds were obscene in the quiet room: slick gliding, muffled moans, the occasional sharp inhale when Beth sucked just right.

Sam rode her face as if she owned it—hips rocking forward and back, then side to side, chasing pressure wherever it felt best. Beth's hands slid up to grip Sam's ass, pulling her down harder, encouraging the rhythm. Sam took the invitation—grinding deeper, faster, smearing herself across Beth's mouth, cheeks, nose, until Beth's face glistened with her fluid.

Beth's tongue never stopped—thrusting inside when Sam tilted her hips just right, lapping broad and hungry when she wanted more surface. Sam's thighs started to tremble, muscles flexing around Beth's head. Her breaths came shorter, sharper—little gasps that turned into low, broken whimpers.

"Look at me," Sam growled suddenly.

Beth's eyes flicked up through damp lash-es—pupils blown, face flushed and shiny, lips swollen and slick. She held Sam's gaze, unflinching, tongue still working relentlessly beneath her.

Sam stared down—eyes half-lidded, lips parted, a feral satisfaction curling her mouth. She looked at Beth like a hunter regarding captured prey: proud, possessive, utterly in control. Like she'd tracked this dangerous, slippery thing through the wild, finally pinned it beneath her, and now she was going to play with it until it broke again.

"You're mine," Sam murmured, voice low and dark, hips rolling slower, more deliberate, dragging out every sensation. "All that mouthy confidence, all those little games you play with everyone else... and here you are, tongue-deep in me, letting me use your face like it's my personal toy."

Beth whimpered against her—vibration ripping another moan from Sam's throat. Her hips stuttered, losing rhythm for a second before she found it again—grinding down harder, chasing the edge.

Beth doubled down—tongue flicking fast over Sam's clit, then sucking hard, fingers digging into Sam's ass to hold her exactly where she needed. Sam's head fell back, a long, shuddering exhale escaping her.

Quiet this time—no scream, no wild cry—just a deep, guttural groan that vibrated through her whole body, she found release, flooding Beth's face with her slime. Her thighs clamped tight around Beth's head, hips jerking in small, helpless pulses as wave after wave rolled through her. She rode it out slow, grinding down one last time, milking every tremor until she was spent.

When the last shudder faded, Sam didn't move right away. She stayed seated—still straddling Beth's face, still holding eye contact—breathing hard, chest rising and falling. That same predatory gleam lingered in her eyes: satisfied, victorious, already thinking about the next time she'd make Beth beg.

Finally, she lifted—just enough to let Beth draw a ragged breath.

Beth's face was a mess—lips red and slick, chin dripping, hair plastered to her forehead with sweat and arousal. She looked up at Sam with dazed, hungry eyes, tongue darting out to lick her swollen lips.

Sam's smirk returned—slow, wicked.

"Good girl," she purred, thumb brushing Beth's cheek, smearing the mess there.

Eventually they stilled—sweat cooling, breaths syncing, bodies heavy.

"You're trouble," Sam murmured.

Beth kissed her temple. "You like it."

Sam huffed a laugh. "Yeah. I really fucking do."

Chapter 20
Same Sam

T he first pale streaks of dawn slipped through the half-open blinds of Sam's bedroom, painting thin gold lines across the tangled sheets and the bare skin of two bodies still wrapped around each other. Sam stirred first—groggy, mouth dry, the faint ache between her thighs a sharp reminder of the night. Beth was sprawled half on top of her, face tucked into the crook of Sam's neck, one leg hooked possessively over Sam's hip, their mixed dark and light hair fanned across shoulders like spilled ink.

Sam blinked against the light, registering the distant murmur of voices from the living room—low, sleepy laughter, the clink of coffee mugs, someone yawning loud enough to carry down the hall. The squad hadn't all left. Half of them were still crashed out there, probably nursing hangovers and swapping stories about last night's chaos.

Sam exhaled slowly, careful not to wake Beth yet. She reached for her phone on the nightstand—6:47 a.m. Shit. Too early for explanations.

She nudged Beth gently. "Hey. Sunrise. We should move."

Beth mumbled something incoherent, burrowing deeper into Sam's chest.

Sam tried again, voice a rough whisper. "Squad's up. They're gonna notice we're both missing. And naked. And in the same bed."

Beth cracked one eye open, squinting at the light. "Let them notice."

Sam sat up a little, sheets pooling at her waist. "Not funny. They'll give me endless shit. 'Same old Sam—only gay when she's drunk.' I can already hear it."

Beth propped herself on an elbow, completely unbothered by her own nakedness. "Then own it." She leaned in, kissed Sam once—lazy, lingering, tasting faintly of last night. "You're not drunk now. And you weren't last night either. Not really."

Sam stared at her, something tight and warm twisting in her chest.

"You like it." Beth rolled out of bed in one fluid motion, stretched—arms overhead, back arching, every line of her body catching the morning light like she was posing for no one in particular and everyone all the same. She grabbed Sam's discarded tank from the floor and tugged it on; it barely skimmed her thighs. "Come on, Captain. Let's give them something to talk about."

Sam hesitated—then swung her legs over the side of the bed, snagged her red panties from the carpet, and pulled them on. She threw on the spirit squad hoodie and zipped it halfway. No bra. No shame.

They padded down the hallway barefoot, hand in hand, not bothering to be quiet.

The living room was a war zone of blankets, empty cans, and half-dressed cheer girls. Jenna was curled on the couch, scrolling through her phone. Debra sat cross-legged on the floor, eating dry cereal straight from the box. Two others—Kayla and Riley—were sprawled across the floor, propped up by the wall, hair still a mess, nursing coffees.

Conversation stopped dead when Sam and Beth appeared in the doorway.

A beat of silence.

Then Jenna's eyes went wide. "Well, well. Look who decided to join the land of the living. We were literally just wondering where Beth went."

Kayla grinned, slow and knowing. "Nah. I bet she did it again. Same old Sam—gets a little tipsy, suddenly remembers she likes girls, hooks up with the new girl on the squad."

Riley laughed into her mug. "Classic. How many times is this now, Sam? Three? Four?"

Sam's jaw tightened, but before she could snap back, Beth stepped forward—still holding her hand, thumb brushing over Sam's knuckles like a quiet claim.

Beth tilted her head, smile easy and dangerous. "I liked it."

The room exploded—gasps, whoops, pillows thrown, someone yelling "DETAILS!" while another chanted "Get it, Captain!"

Beth laughed—bright, unapologetic—and tugged Sam down onto the couch beside her. Sam let herself be pulled, settling against Beth's side, arm automatically draping over her shoulders.

The teasing kept coming—light, relentless, the kind of shit only a squad could dish out without malice.

Sam exhaled, tension easing out of her shoulders for the first time that morning.

Sunlight poured stronger through the windows now, warming the room, catching the glitter of spilled seltzer on the coffee table, the tangle of limbs and laughter.

Last night was over, and Beth's mind quickly turned back to the school and all the leverage she was quickly building. She now had a very powerful alliance forming around her, just in time for the next phase of her plan.

Chapter 21
Jail Bait

Monday morning hit like a slap of cold air. Beth was already halfway to school, sneakers scuffing the cracked sidewalk, when she pulled out her phone and fired off the text without breaking stride.

She hit send, then slipped the phone back into her hoodie pocket. A slow, dark smile curled her mouth as she pictured his face when he read it—confused, hopeful, already half-hard just from her name popping up on his screen.

The reply came thirty seconds later.

Beth didn't answer right away. She kept walking, breath fogging in the crisp air, but inside her chest something hot and vicious uncoiled.

The thought of him waiting—nervous, eager, completely unaware she was already three moves ahead—sent a shiver straight down her spine, pooling low in her belly. Her thighs clenched involuntarily. She bit her lip hard enough to taste copper, imagining the way his hands would shake when he finally touched her, the way he'd look at her like she was the only thing that mattered.

She nearly came right there on the sidewalk—fully clothed, no hands, just the sheer mental rush of control. Evil, pure and electric, fizzing through her veins like bad champagne. She laughed under her breath, low and private, and kept walking.

The batting cages were tucked behind the gym, chain-link fences rattling faintly in the breeze. Benny was already there—leaning against the fence in his usual black hoodie and jeans, hands shoved deep in his pockets, looking like he hadn't slept much. When he saw her, he straightened fast, a shy half-smile breaking across his face.

"Hey," he said.

Beth didn't smile back. She walked straight up to him, stopped just close enough that their shoes touched, and looked at him through her lashes with deliberate coolness.

"Hey, yourself."

He shifted, uncertain. "You okay? You sounded... busy."

She didn't answer. Just stepped closer—slow, deliberate—until her chest brushed his. Then she waited.

Benny hesitated another second before his arms came around her, tentative at first, then tighter. He hugged her like he was afraid she'd vanish if he squeezed too hard.

Beth pressed her face into the side of his neck, lips grazing skin. She exhaled, slow and hot, letting her breath ghost over his pulse point.

He shuddered.

"Let's skip," she whispered against his throat.

"Huh?" His voice cracked.

"Let's skip school."

Benny pulled back just enough to look at her. "No, I can't. If we get caught, my sister will find out about us."

"I know," she murmured, sliding her cold hands up his back under the hoodie, nails dragging lightly. "That makes it even more fucking hot."

She rolled her pelvis forward—subtle—rubbing herself against his thigh in one slow grind.

He sucked in a sharp breath.

"Alright," he said, half-laughing, half-dazed. "But it better be good."

Beth thought for a moment. "Have you ever been to a hotel party before?"

"No," he replied, looking at her with curiosity.

"We used to do it all the time at my old school," she said, another smooth lie. "Trust me. It's fun."

He rubbed the back of his neck. "We can take my truck. If you've got a license."

"Yeah, Benny, of course I do, I'm eighteen."

He took her word for it, forgetting to—or rather, absentmindedly, not asking to check.

They walked the three blocks to his house in easy silence, shoulders brushing. When they reached the driveway, he glanced toward the windows—curtains still drawn, no cars in sight.

"My mom is always home," he muttered, "we gotta be quiet."

They snuck around the side, through the gate, to where his beat-up little old Ford Ranger sat under a tarp in the back. He pulled the keys from his pocket with shaky fingers.

"It ain't much, but it's my first ride."

"It's cute," Beth teased.

"Take it slow," he said, half-joking, half-serious.

Beth slid into the passenger seat, legs spread just enough to make her sweats ride up her crotch. "I will," she promised, voice dripping honey. "Slow as you want, Benny boy." She slammed the door shut.

They drove a few minutes to the nearest hotel—the kind with weekly rates and a blatant vacancy that clearly spoke to the few guests as if to say, 'We don't know how we afford this place either.' Still well kept, she pulled the truck into the valet, handing the attendant five dollars like it was a golden ticket. Beth hopped out first, sauntered to the front desk like she owned the place.

She folded a credit card into a twenty-dollar bill and handed it over so slyly that Benny never even saw the exchange. The clerk barely looked up; he handed her a keycard for room 216 without asking for ID.

Benny waited by the truck, fidgeting.

She dangled the key in front of him when she got back. "We should hit the pool first. But we need outfits. There's an outlet store across the street."

They crossed the road laughing—her arm looped through his, his shoulders finally relaxing. At the gas station next to the outlet, she popped into the gift shop while he waited outside.

"Be right back," she called.

Two minutes later, she emerged with a pack of Marlboro cigarettes and a cheap lighter. She tore the cellophane, tapped one out, and offered it to him.

"First time?" she asked, lighting her own.

He took it with unsteady fingers. "Yeah."

He struggled to light his. Beth laughed delightfully, watching the wind blow out the flame of the lighter. Benny inhaled a dry toke—coughed hard—then tried again. Beth leaned over, cupping her hands around the flame as they stepped off the curb. She almost fell over with laughter herself at the screeching brakes and the blaring horn when he nearly walked out into traffic trying to light it for the third time.

"Careful, killer," she teased, tugging him back by his hoodie. "Don't get yourself killed. I'm not done with you yet."

Time seemed to skip as they walked, almost as if they were skipping too—funny how that happens when you skip school. They finished smoking on the curb, shoulders touching, trading drags and dumb jokes. When the cigarettes were stubs she stubbed hers out and grabbed his hand.

"Come on. Bathing suits."

Inside the outlet store, she dragged him toward the swimwear racks. She picked a black string bikini for herself—tiny triangles, barely-there ties—and a pair of red board shorts for him.

"Try these," she said, shoving them into his arms. "I'll be in the changing room."

She disappeared behind the curtain. A second later, her voice floated out.

"Benny? Come in here. Hold my stuff."

He hesitated—glanced around—then slipped inside.

The changing room was narrow, with a mirror on one wall. She handed him her hoodie and shorts, then turned her back.

"Turn around," she ordered, playful but firm. "No peeking."

He faced the curtain, heart hammering.

She shimmied out of her clothes—fabric rustling, soft exhales. In the mirror, he couldn't help it—he flicked his eyes sideways. The angle was shit; all he could see was her ass.

The string bikini bottom slid up her thighs, the ties dangling loose against her hips as she tied them. She bent slightly to adjust the top, breasts swaying, and he nearly groaned out loud.

She caught his reflection in the mirror—eyes dark, lips parted—and smirked.

"Bad boy," she whispered. "You peeked."

He swallowed. "Couldn't help it."

She turned, bikini barely covering anything, and stepped close enough that her bare stomach brushed his shirt.

"Pool," she said.

Benny nodded—speechless, already hard, already gone.

Beth put her clothes on over the bikini and shoved the trunk into Ben's pants. She looked around the ridges of the ceiling for cameras. "Come on," she said, grabbing his hand, leading him out of the booth. "Run."

Chapter 22

Hoe Hoe Hotel

They spent the day by the pool like it was their own private kingdom.

The hotel pool water was warm from the midday sun—warm enough for an autumn day anyway. A handful of other guests—mostly small families passing through—kept to the shallow end or the lounge chairs under faded umbrellas.

Benny floated near the far corner, arms draped over the edge, legs kicking lazily in the water while he watched the surface ripple. Beth had slipped out a few minutes earlier, towel wrapped around her waist, promising she'd be right back.

She reappeared at the poolside bar, chatting easily with the bored bartender. A quick flash of the fake ID—a glossy driver's license with a photo of some girl who vaguely resembled her if you squinted—and two plastic cups appeared, sweating with cheap vodka and clear soda. Beth brought them back to their side of the pool and handed one to Benny.

She slid into the water beside him, the surface breaking around her hips. "Don't worry, Benjamin," she said, handing him one of the cups with a grin. Ice clinked softly against the plastic as he took it. "I've got us covered."

He raised an eyebrow, glancing at the drink, then back at her. "You're gonna get us kicked out before we even finish these."

Beth laughed low, clinking her cup against his. "Only if we're loud about it." She took a sip, eyes bright over the rim, then leaned back against the pool wall next to him, shoulders brushing in the warm water.

Benny stared at it, then at her, then back at the ID. "You're terrifying."

She laughed—bright, sharp. "Drink up."

They got drunk outside near the pool, day-drunk in the lazy, golden way that makes everything feel slow and inevitable. Beth's stringy bikini clung to her like wet ink; Benny's red board shorts rode low on his hips. They floated on cheap inflatable rings, passed the cup back and forth, kissing sloppily and laughing when no one was looking. The sun climbed higher, turning their skin pink, the vodka turning their edges soft and reckless.

Beth finished her drink and climbed out of the pool, water trickling down her body. "Come on, let's go to the room."

Benny followed her up to the hotel room, both of them leaving a glistening trail across the lobby tile. Water dripped from Beth's soaked hair in steady plinks, pooling in small dark spots behind her bare feet; Benny's board shorts slapped wetly against his thighs with every step, the sound echoing off the cheap tile. A bored desk clerk glanced up from his phone, eyebrows lifting for half a second at the sight of two dripping teenagers, then looked right back down like he'd seen worse.

In the elevator, Beth leaned against the mirrored wall, arms crossed over the towel so her bikini would dry quicker. A single drop slid from her collarbone, traced a slow path between her breasts, and disappeared under the fabric of her bottoms. Benny stood opposite her, hands gripping his towel as to keep it around his waist. The mirrored walls threw back their reflections in endless repetition: her smirking at him, him trying (and failing) not to stare at the way water beaded on her thighs and ran in fine lines down her legs.

The elevator dinged. Doors slid open on the second floor.

Beth stepped out first, hips swaying, leaving wet footprints on the hallway carpet that darkened in perfect outlines of her toes. Benny followed close—close enough to smell chlorine on her skin—and when she paused at room 216 to swipe the keycard, he pressed against her back just enough to let her feel how much he wanted her.

The lock clicked green.

She pushed the door open and glanced back at him over her shoulder, water still dripping from her neck.

"After you," she said, voice low, teasing. "Unless you'd rather stand in the hall and drip some more."

Benny swallowed, stepped inside, and the door clicked shut behind them—locking out the hallway, the lobby, and the rest of the world.

Chapter 23

You, Me, and Marriott

B enny sat on the edge of the bed, still damp from the pool, red board shorts clinging to his thighs. The vodka buzz hummed low in his veins, warm and loose,

Beth stepped into the room black bikini top peeking from beneath the towel. Her hair, now dark and slick, still dripping; she grabbed her makeup bag from it quickly, and then threw her backpack down against the wall—her clothes a not-so-important idea compared to what she had in mind.

She dropped onto the bed beside him, legs immediately draping across his lap, bare thighs pressing against his damp shorts.

She leaned in and kissed him once—they tasted of sweet lipstick and sour vodka. She pulled back and unzipped her makeup bag.

Inside: a tiny baggie of white powder, a cut-down straw, the hotel keycard, and a compact mirror.

Benny's stomach flipped. "Beth…"

"Relax." She dumped a small pile onto the mirror, tapped it into two neat lines with the edge of the keycard. "Just a little fun. You've never done this before?"

He shook his head.

She looked up at him—eyes dark, pupils already wide from the booze and the anticipation. "First time for everything."

She bent over the mirror first—hair falling forward, ass lifting slightly off the bed as she snorted the line in one smooth pull. She sat back, licked her gums, and shivered once like electricity had run through her.

"Your turn," she said, holding the mirror out.

Benny hesitated. Then he leaned in—awkward, nervous—and mimicked her. The burn hit his sinuses like fire; he coughed, eyes watering. Beth laughed softly, rubbing his back in slow circles.

"Good boy," she purred.

Already, the rush had begun. Slamming through him sharp and bright, making every breath feel electric.

She straddled his lap right there on the bed. "Truth or dare?"

"Truth."

"Oh, come on, wimp."

He looked up at her in his lap with tired eyes.

"Oh, fine, you want the truth?"

He blinked at her softly.

"The rumors are true." She bit her lip. "I did hook up with Alex."

"No, no, not that," Benny said, a flare in his eye, but she played dumb, looking back at him with a forced look of confusion.

"Why did you transfer?"

"Huh?" She paused for a moment and pondered his eyes. "What do you mean?"

"I mean what I said. Why did you transfer?"

"I moved here."

"No, you didn't."

They sat quietly for a second, the coke still buzzing, making the quiet feel alive.

She peered deep into his eyes, forcing them to connect their gaze and causing their breathing to synchronize, the room quiet except for the low hum of the AC.

She looked at him blindly for a moment longer. "Yeah, Benny, I did. Now come on, say dare!"

He swallowed. "Dare."

She smiled—slow, wicked. "Let's take a shower together."

Benny shifted, propping himself on one elbow. "I have to get home before my parents wonder why I didn't come home," he said, voice rough, strained.

Beth's hand slid up his chest, fingers curling around the back of his neck. She leaned in over him, lips brushing his ear.

He exhaled hard. "Beth…"

"Stay a bit longer, Benny," she whispered, voice low and needy again. "Just a little longer. Don't you want to take a shower with me?"

"Alright, fine, but then I have to go."

"Okay. Let me get my clothes from my bag," she peeped out excitedly. "Oh my, I almost forgot!" she said suddenly, reaching deep into her backpack.

Chapter 24
Beth's New Toy

The late-afternoon sun slanted through the half-drawn blinds of the hotel room, turning the narrow space golden and lazy. A half-eaten bag of sour gummies sat open on the bed. Benny sat on the edge of the mattress—knees spread, elbows on thighs, looking every bit the polite, slightly nervous brother who was the perfect naive mirror of his older sister, Lainey.

Beth rose off the other bed to shut the curtains, bringing the mood to a cool, more sensual feel.

She moved ike she had all the time in the world. She turned back toward him, kicked off her sneakers, peeled the oversized hoodie over her head (revealing a thin white tank underneath, no bra, nipples already faintly visible through the cotton), then placed herself standing between his knees at the edge of the bed, looking down at him with a blinkered pout.

"You're tense," she said, voice soft, almost concerned. "You don't have to be. I'm not gonna bite." A small smile. "Unless you ask."

Benny laughed—short, a little awkward.

Beth tilted her head, hair falling over one shoulder. She reached behind her, and pulled a small black velvet pouch out of the dresser. She held it between two fingers, letting it dangle.

"I brought a little something, Benny," she murmured.

His eyes flicked to the pouch, then back to her face. Throat worked. "What is it?"

She loosened the drawstring with slow tugs, tipped the contents into her palm: a smooth, curved pink dildo, small at the tip, flaring wider at the base. She rolled it between her fingers like it was nothing more than a pretty toy.

"Just a little toy," she said innocently. "I like how it feels, but I can never get the angle right by myself." She met his eyes, wide and guileless. "You've got nice hands. Strong. Steady. You could do it for me. Will you put it inside me? Please?"

Benny stared at the toy, then at her. His cheeks were already flushing. "Beth…"

She leaned forward just enough that the tank gaped slightly, giving him a clear view down the front. "It's okay if you say no. I won't be mad." Her voice dropped softer. "But I'd really like it if you said yes."

He exhaled hard through his nose. Looked away for a second—toward the door, toward the window—then back to her. "You're trouble."

"I know." She smiled, sweet and slow. "That's why you keep coming back for more."

He hesitated another beat. Then he reached out, fingers brushing hers as he took it from her hand. It looked small in his palm, but the weight of it seemed to change everything.

Beth gave him a slow, teasing smile—the kind that started at her lips and spread like wildfire through her eyes. She stood up from the bed in one fluid motion, fingers already hooking under the hem of her thin white tank. She didn't rush. She let the moment stretch, let him feel every second of anticipation.

Her nipples peaked through the tank top, dark against the pale swell of the shirt. She turned slowly, giving him the full view—back first, the shirt riding up enough to show the dimples at the base of her spine, the gentle flare of her hips. Then she faced him again, fingers playing with the hem.

Ben sat frozen on the edge of the bed, hands braced on his thighs, eyes wide and dark. His breath had gone shallow; she could see the pulse jumping in his throat, the way his fingers flexed like he wasn't sure whether to reach for her or hold himself back.

Beth hooked her thumbs into the waistband of her shorts—simple black cotton. She tugged them down in one unhurried motion, letting the fabric drag along the tops of her thighs and over the curve of her ass. The shorts pooled at her ankles; she stepped out of them with a small, deliberate lift of each foot, and then kicked them aside without breaking eye contact.

Now only the panties remained—black cheeky briefs, high-cut on the sides, clinging to her like a second skin. The lace trim along the edges was already darkened from moisture soaking through. She let her fingers trace the waistband for a moment—teasing the elastic, snapping it lightly against her hip—before sliding them down too.

She bent slightly at the waist as she pushed them lower. The panties slid down her thighs, catching briefly at the fullest part before she straightened out, letting them fall in pillowed surrender, drifting down her legs like weightless rose petals.

She stepped free, bare feet silent on the carpet. Completely naked now except for the undershirt that barely skimmed the top of her pelvis. She stood there—legs slightly parted, skin flushed. A thin trail of wetness glistened on her inner thigh; she didn't bother hiding it.

Ben's mouth parted. No sound came out at first—just a rough exhale, like the air had been punched out of him. His hands gripped his own thighs harder, knuckles whitening. His eyes roamed helplessly: Her nipples peering back at him through the thin cotton, the soft curve of her stomach, the shadowed space between her legs where she was visibly slick and swollen.

"Jesus, Beth..." His voice cracked on her name—low, reverent, almost pained.

She stepped closer—close enough that her bare knees brushed his denim jeans. The heat radiating off her body washed over him. She leaned down, palms sliding up his chest to rest on his shoulders, fingers curling into the fabric of his shirt.

"Still think you have to leave?" she whispered, lips brushing the shell of his ear. "Or are you finally going to touch what you've been staring at?"

Ben's hands finally moved—slow at first, like he was afraid she'd vanish if he went too fast. His palms settled on her hips, thumbs stroking the sensitive skin just above the flare of her ass. He pulled her forward gently, guiding her to straddle his lap again, the hard length of him pressing up against her through his pants.

She rocked once. A soft moan slipped from her throat.

Ben groaned against her neck, hands sliding up under the shirt to cup her breasts, thumbs brushing her nipples in slow circles.

"I'm not going anywhere," he rasped, voice thick with want. "Not until you tell me to."

Beth smiled against his mouth—slow, triumphant.

Benny had almost forgotten how to breathe. His eyes roamed—hungry, reverent—taking in the faint freckles across her collarbone, the love bite still blooming purple on the side of her neck from last week, the slick shine between her thighs stuck to his.

"Fuck," he whispered, almost to himself.

Stood again, for a moment between his knees, hands sliding into his hair, tilting his face up to meet her gaze. She smiled—slow, victorious—she took small, precise strides to the other side of the room and sat down on the other bed. She arched her back slightly as she leaned back and presented her thighs open. She motioned a finger for him to come over to her.

"I'm so... wet," she whispered.

Benny swallowed audibly. His free hand hovered, then settled on her hip—tentative at first, then firmer, thumb stroking the soft skin there.

"I need it inside me. Put it inside me, Benny."

He made a low sound in his throat—half groan, half surrender. His fingers tightened on her hip. The toy was still in his other hand, cool against her skin when he finally primed the tip to enter her.

She sighed—long, relieved—as he slowly pushed it inside her. Inch by inch. The stretch was perfect; she rocked back to meet it, taking more.

"Good boy," she breathed, lost in his grasp with ecstasy, feeling the toy glide and shift inside her with every movement.

Beth smiled, slow and wicked, grinding down once more so he could feel exactly how full she was, and just how much she enjoyed it.

Chapter 25

Let It Reign

Beth woke up, realizing that they both dozed off for a while. She shook him off of her in an attempt to wake him. "Benny, how 'bout that shower now?"

"Huh? Yeah, sure," he said, half asleep and still rather unaware.

He woke more with every light and sound: the click from the TV when she turned it on, the spewing of the faucet when she turned it on, and now the running of the water.

Beth's voice floated out—playful, echoing off the tiles. "Aren't you going to join me?"

Benny got up from the bed in a rush, heart slamming against his ribs. He crept to the bathroom door—hasty, clumsy, bare feet silent on the thin carpet—and pushed it open wider. The fogged mirror caught his reflection for a split second: flushed cheeks, wide eyes, hair still damp from the pool. Then the steam hit him like a warm wave, thick and enveloping.

The overhead light shone through the translucent shower curtain, turning her silhouette into something dreamlike—curves blurred, movement fluid. A towel hung carelessly on the hook nearby.

She opened the curtain with one slow tug.

"There you are," she said. Water streamed down her naked body—over her shoulders, between her breasts, and down the flat plane of her stomach.

Benny watched, frozen, mesmerized by the drips rolling from her smooth pelvic mound.

She twirled under the spray—slow, deliberate—head tipping back so the water sluiced over her throat, her collarbone, the swell of her ass. She ran her hands slowly up her body—palms flat against her stomach, then higher, cupping her breasts, thumbs brushing her nipples until they peaked.

She laughed—low, throaty, menacing in its delight—and turned so her back was to him. She braced one hand on the wall, arched slightly, letting the water pound down her spine while her other hand slid between her legs. Slow circles. Deliberate. Her hips rolled once, twice, a soft moan slipping out that cut right through him.

Her breathing had gone ragged now—shallow, needy gasps that echoed off the wet tiles. The teasing edge in her voice had melted into something rawer, hungrier. She glanced back over her shoulder through the steam, eyes glassy and half-lidded, lips parted on another shaky exhale. "Are you getting in... or what?" she managed, the words coming out broken and breathy—half plea, half whine. Her fingers kept moving, slower now, trembling as she circled her clit again. "Please, Benny... I need you in here. I'm so fucking wet, and it's not enough... come touch me... please..."

The sound of her—needy, almost desperate plea—snapped something in him.

Benny's mouth went dry. "Yeah."

He fumbled with his soaked board shorts—hands shaking, fingers clumsy from nerves and the lingering coke rush. The drawstring knot refused to give at first; he cursed under his breath, yanking harder. The fabric finally gave, sliding down his thighs in a wet slap. He kicked them off, nearly tripping over them in the process.

Beth laughed—a bright folly, a choked shine of joy in her every groan.

"Jesus, Benny," she teased, eyes sparkling through the steam. "You undress like it's your first time. Cute."

He flushed harder, cock already hard and bobbing as he stepped under the spray.

She kept teasing—fingers moving lazily between her legs, head tipped back so the water streamed over her face, lips parted. Every so often, she'd glance over her shoulder through the steam, eyes locking on his with every other glance.

She turned fully toward him now, water rushing down her front side, nipples hard from the heat and the tease. "Come closer," she said finally, voice husky.

He did.

She pressed herself against him—wet skin on wet skin, breasts flattening against his chest, her thigh sliding between his. His cock sprang back harder, aching as she trapped it against her stomach. She wrapped her fingers around it, stroking it firmly while the water pounded over them both.

"Truth or dare?" she whispered against his lips.

"Dare," he rasped.

She smiled—slow, wicked—pushing down on his shoulders, forcing him to his knees.

Benny sank willingly, water streaming into his eyes, down his face. She stood over him—legs parted, one hand braced on the wall above his head, the other sliding into his wet hair. She tugged his face forward until his mouth was level with her pussy lips.

"Eat me," she ordered, voice low and commanding. "Like you mean it."

He hesitated at first.

His hands gripped the backs of her thighs—fingers digging into soft, wet flesh—as he pressed his mouth to her. Tongue flat and broad, he licked a long, slow stripe. The taste of her, like salt and caramel. She moaned—deep, satisfied—and rolled her hips forward, grinding against his face.

"Peasant," she breathed under her breath.

His lips closed around her clit, sucking gently at first, then harder, creating a seal as his licks became more rhythmic. His tongue flicked fast, then slow circles, then flat. She rocked against him—slow, filthy—using his mouth like she owned it. Water poured over his head, down his back, mixing with the slickness coating his chin, his lips.

Beth's fingers tightened in his hair—pulling, guiding, holding him exactly where she wanted. Her thighs trembled around his ears. Her breaths became shorter, sharper—little gasps that turned into broken whimpers.

"Look at your queen," she growled with lust.

He tilted his head up—eyes watering from the spray, face glistening, meeting her gaze through the haze of the moment. She stared down at him with a feral satisfaction in her aura.

"You're so good at this," she purred, hips rolling faster. "My sweet, eager little Benny… on his knees where he belongs."

He groaned against her—vibration ripping another moan from her throat. His tongue never stopped—thrusting inside when she tilted her hips just right, lapping broad and hungry when she wanted more surface.

"Put your fingers in."

He slid one hand up her thigh, his fingers joining his mouth at first—then sliding them deep into her, his tongue whipped her clit relentlessly, his fingers found a bulb and curled forward on it, matching the same rhythm now.

Her moaning stopped; she started again with a brand new tone. Quiet at first, then louder—a low, shuddering cry that echoed more and more. Her thighs clamped around his head, hips jerking.

She shattered—pulse after pulse, wave after wave, rolling through her.

When the last shudder faded, she didn't let him up right away. She kept him there—still on his knees, mouth pressed to her oversensitive folds—breathing hard, chest rising and falling.

Finally, she tugged him up by the hair—gentle but firm.

He rose on shaky legs, cock throbbing painfully between them.

She kissed him—deep—tasting herself on his tongue.

"Good boy," she whispered against his mouth. "Now go home."

Chapter 26

On a Tuesday?

The next morning arrived like a quick cold flash of fluorescent light on her reality of fun short weekends and long drawn weeks of drama; she couldn't cut class every day, could she? Beth walked the halls with her chin up, sporting her cheer tank and shorts with pride, complemented nonetheless by the bob of her high ponytail.

The hallways felt quieter than usual, the post-weekend gossip having cooled into background noise. Even the squad's morning check-in by the lockers was routine—Jenna complaining about her parents, Kayla scrolling her phone, Sam barking reminders about Friday's conditioning session. Beth nodded along, smiled in the right places, let her fingers brush Sam's wrist once when no one was looking—a quick, secret reminder of her—then drifted on.

Most of the day was oddly normal. Classes dragged in their usual rhythm—teachers droning through slides, pens scratching notes, the occasional cough or phone buzz breaking the monotony. Beth moved through it all with practiced ease: raising her hand just enough to look engaged without drawing too much attention, laughing at the right moments in group discussions. Beth slipped out of study hall with her usual vague excuse—"Cheer stuff, gotta grab something from the gym"—and drifted into the corridors like she belonged nowhere in particular.

The halls smelled faintly of floor wax and old textbooks. Lockers stood silent, fluorescent lights buzzed overhead. She was halfway to the vending machines when she rounded the corner and nearly collided with Alex.

He was coming the other way—football playbook tucked under one arm, hoodie sleeves pushed up to his elbows, hair still damp from morning practice. He stopped short, eyes flicking over her in that quick, instinctive way he always did: assessing, wary, a little hungry despite himself.

They shared a strange glance—longer than polite, shorter than comfortable. The air between them thickened.

"Alex Harding, star quarterback." Beth tilted her head, ponytail swinging. "Heading to the weight room?"

"Yeah. Coach wants us to review film before lunch." He shifted his weight, grip tightening on the playbook. "You?"

She shrugged one shoulder. "Just wandering. Study hall is boring."

A beat passed. Neither moved.

Alex cleared his throat. "You look... good."

Beth's mouth curved—just the corner. "Thanks. You too. Still got that post-practice glow."

He huffed a small laugh, rubbing the back of his neck. "Yeah. Sweaty glow."

She stepped closer—casual, like she was just adjusting her bag strap. Close enough that he could smell her coconut shampoo and pineapple body wash. "You ever think about me?" she asked softly.

Alex's jaw ticked. "Beth..."

She didn't let him finish. She reached past him to the water fountain, bending slowly to take a drink—back arched just enough, shorts riding up her thighs. When she straightened, water glistened on her lower lip. She licked it away deliberately.

Alex's eyes tracked the motion.

She turned to face him fully. "You're staring."

"You're making it hard not to."

Beth smiled—slow, knowing. "Come on, Alex. No one's around."

She took his wrist—gentle but firm—and tugged him a few steps to the door of the boys' bathroom. She pushed it open with her hip, pulled him inside.

🌂

Alex exhaled hard. "Beth, stop."

She pressed against him—chest to chest, hips rocking forward so he could feel how warm she was through her shorts. "You know you want it. Look—it's just us. No one has to know."

His hands came up to her waist—half to push her away, half to feel her figure. "No. I can't trust you."

Beth laughed softly—low, throaty. "Come on. You know girls like me, Alex, we just want to have fun.

His eyes doubled around a few times. "You gonna go off on me again? Start some scene in the cafeteria?"

She shook her head, fingers sliding up his hoodie to rest over his heart. "Let's be honest. I was just new to the school and... I thought you actually liked me. But now I'm back to my old ways—just looking for a toy to play with."

Alex's breath hitched. "I'm sure you are."

She dragged him deeper into the room—back against the sink—then turned them so he was the one pinned. Her hands were already under his hoodie, palms flat against his stomach, nails dragging lightly down to the waistband of his sweats.

He groaned—low, defeated—and kissed her.

It was messy, hungry, teeth clashing. His mouth found her neck. She let a need moan, her fingers working the drawstring of his sweats, shoving them down just enough.

He lifted her onto the sink edge—cold porcelain serving goosebumps through her sheer cotton shorts. She wrapped her legs around his waist, pulling him closer. His sweats tangled around, falling to his ankles. He kicked them off impatiently. She reached into his boxers, guiding him—hot, hard, already leaking—until he pushed inside in one slow, deep thrust.

They both gasped.

Her hips snapped forward. The sink rattled with every thrust—porcelain clinking against tile. Her smooth skin, his rough skin. She dug her nails deeper into his chest, urging him to go faster, harder. He obliged—grunting against her throat, one hand braced on the wall beside her head, the other gripping her thigh so tight it'd bruise.

"Fuck—Beth—"

She clenched around him, deliberate and mean.

"This is so hot," she demanded, voice wrecked, "we could get caught right now."

Alex stopped.

"No, don't stop," Beth pleaded.

The bell for lunch rang like any other.

Chapter 27
Splitting Hairs

At lunch, she found Benny first.

Beth caught Benny's eye across the cafeteria—he was slouched in the back corner, hoodie up, looking like he hadn't slept. When their gazes locked, he blushed and dropped his head, shoveling food into his mouth like he didn't want to see her.

Beth smiled to herself, small and private.

He was sitting alone at the edge of the bench. He picked at his sandwich, pretending like he wasn't watching her walk straight toward him.

She dropped her bag on the table and straddled the bench, taking a seat next to him—knees brushing his.

"Hey, stranger," she said, voice low.

Benny glanced around—nervous, guilty—then back at her. "Beth... Lainey's gonna kill me if she sees us."

"Then don't let her see." She leaned in and brushed her lips against his ear. "Miss me?"

He swallowed hard. "Yeah."

When she pulled back, she noticed someone standing over them across the bench.

Beth felt Benny stiffen beneath her hands. She turned her head slowly, lazily, like she had all the time in the world.

A boy stood there—tall and wide. He wore a faded shirt, cargo shorts, and skateboard sneakers that looked like they were unfamiliar with the sport. His backpack hung off one shoulder; he'd clearly been ready to sit until he noticed her.

His mouth was open. Not dramatically—just a small stun of recognition and disbelief.

Benny made a strangled sound in his throat.

"Uh... hey, Brian," he managed, voice cracking on the last syllable.

Brian blinked once. Twice. Then his gaze flicked from Benny's flushed face to Beth—still leaning over his lap, ponytail swinging slightly from the sudden turn.

"Yo," Brian said finally, voice cracking higher than he probably wanted. "Am I... interrupting something?"

Beth tilted her head, studying him like a mildly interesting specimen. Then she smiled—slow, sweet, and utterly unapologetic.

"Ta-ta," she said brightly, sliding off Benny's lap in one fluid motion. She adjusted her shorts with a casual tug, bent down to brush a final kiss against Benny's temple—soft, possessive—and whispered something into his ear so only he could hear.

She straightened, gave Brian a little finger-wave that was equal parts playful and dismissive, grabbed her backpack from the bench, and walked away without looking back. Her hips swayed just enough to make sure both boys watched every step until she disappeared around the corner into the courtyard.

Silence stretched.

Brian finally exhaled, long and shaky.

"Dude," he said, dropping onto the bench across from Benny like his legs had given out. "That was... Beth? The transfer girl? The one with the rumors and the cheer squad and the—holy shit, man."

Benny dragged both hands down his face in dread. "Yeah..."

Brian leaned forward, elbows on the table, staring at Benny like he'd grown a second head.

"You're hooking up with her? Like... actually hooking up?"

Benny nodded once—miserable, exhilarated, terrified all at once.

Brian let out a low whistle. "Bro. She's, like... nuclear. Everyone's talking about her."

Benny looked down at his untouched sandwich. "I don't know what I'm doing, man."

"You're telling me. She just kissed you in public, letting everyone know that she owns you. And you let her."

Brian studied him for a long beat—concern creeping in behind the shock.

"You okay? Like... really okay?"

Benny exhaled hard. "No. Yes. I don't know. She's... she's everywhere. And I can't stop thinking about her. But Lainey's gonna murder me if she finds out."

Brian winced. "Yeah. Your sister's already on high alert. She asked me yesterday if I'd seen you 'acting weird.' I lied. Badly."

Benny groaned. "Great."

Brian leaned back, arms crossed. "So what's the plan? You gonna keep sneaking around until she catches you? Or are you actually gonna tell her? She's gonna find out."

Benny stared at the table. "I don't know. Beth says we're just... having fun. That it doesn't have to be complicated."

Brian snorted. "Yeah, because Beth's the queen of uncomplicated," he said with a sarcastic strain.

Benny didn't argue.

Brian sighed. "Look, man. I'm not gonna narc. But be careful. She's got a reputation for a reason."

Benny met his eyes with a flickering stare.

"I know," he said quietly. "But I can't stop."

Brian didn't have an answer for that.

The bell rang.

Brian stood and slung his backpack over his shoulder. "Just... don't get yourself expelled. Or heartbroken. Or both."

Benny managed a weak laugh. "No promises."

Brian hesitated, then clapped him on the shoulder—harder than necessary, like he was trying to shake sense into him.

"See you in class," he said, and walked off.

Benny sat there alone for another minute, heart and mind still racing.

Freshly fueled from her lunch drama with Benny and his friend, Beth stayed cool, playing buddy with Lainey, who sat two seats over. She waited until the teacher turned to the whiteboard, then leaned across the aisle.

"Hey," she said softly. "You okay?"

Lainey didn't look at her. "Fine."

Beth nudged her sneaker under the desk. "What's wrong?"

Lainey finally turned—eyes glossed. "You have any idea why my brother came home late last night?"

Beth's expression softened—just enough. "Uh, no, Benny?"

Lainey exhaled through her nose. "Forgive me for saying this, but you weren't in class yesterday, so I thought maybe you had something to do with it."

"No," Beth said, and she even sounded like she meant it. "I had a dental appointment. See, all clean," she said, grinning her teeth and pointing at them.

Lainey studied her for a long beat, then rolled her eyes.

"You don't believe me, bestie?"

Lainey didn't look convinced, but she let it drop.

"Seriously, Beth, stay away from him."

Chapter 28

Locker Room Lovers

Beth made her way to gym class and found the squad was already stretching on the mats, music thumping low. Sam was at the front, arms crossed, watching them with that sharp captain stare.

Beth walked in like she owned the place.

Jenna spotted her first. "There she is."

The others laughed—easy, teasing.

Riley snorted. "High standards. Like Sam."

"What are you guys talking about?" Beth questioned as she approached.

Samantha interjected, "Enough gossip. Warm up. We've got regionals in three weeks."

Sam shot Beth a look—half warning, half amused. Beth met her gaze across the mat, held it a beat too long. Sam's mouth curved—just the corner—then she clapped once.

They fell into routine—stretches, basics, stunts. Beth moved through it seamlessly, catching Sam's eye every time they reset a pyramid, letting her fingers brush Sam's waist when no one was looking.

After practice, the locker room hummed with the usual post-workout chaos—metal doors slamming, laughter echoing off tile, the sharp scent of body spray mixing with sweat and soap. One by one, the girls filed out. Their voices faded down the hallway until the room settled into a softer quiet—only the occasional drip from a faucet and the low buzz of the overhead lights.

Beth lingered by her locker, pretending to reorganize her bag, rolling her ankle slowly like she was checking for soreness. She watched the others disappear through the door, waving casual goodbyes, until the space felt almost empty.

Almost.

She glanced around. Sam wasn't at her locker. Wasn't by the mirrors fixing her ponytail. Wasn't grabbing her water bottle from the bench.

There was only one place she could be.

The showers.

Perfect.

☂

Beth couldn't help but smile. She slung her towel over her shoulder, kicked off her sneakers, and padded barefoot across the cool tile toward the arched entryway that led to the communal shower stalls. Steam still drifted lazily from the open area, carrying the faint scent of Sam's eucalyptus body wash.

She slipped inside, the humid air wrapping around her like a warm hand.

Sam stood under the last showerhead, back turned, water streaming down the long line of her spine, wrapping around her curves, and rushing through the smooth valleys of her body. The water pooled at her feet in admiration before swirling down the drain. Her head was tipped back, eyes closed, letting the spray pound against her neck and shoulders, washing away the day's tension.

Beth leaned against the tiled wall just outside the direct spray, arms crossed, watching for a quiet moment.

She quickly discarded her clothes, then she spoke—voice low, teasing.

"Waiting for me, Captain?"

Sam turned her head quickly—halfway spooked, halfway confused.

Beth reached up and brushed a damp strand of hair off Sam's forehead. "Care to practice a new routine?"

Sam caught her wrist—gentle but firm. "Beth, not here."

Beth's smile was slow, wicked. "Why not? Everyone's gone."

She twisted her wrist free slowly, then slid both hands up Sam's arms—palms gliding, fingers tracing. Sam exhaled sharply when Beth rubbed the undersides of her breasts, thumbs circling her nipples without mercy.

"Beth—"

"Shh." Beth pressed closer—bodies aligning under the spray, wet skin sliding against wet skin. She tilted her head, lips grazing Sam's jaw. "You've been tense all practice. Let me fix it."

Sam's hands came up defensively, then settled on Beth's hips. "You're gonna get us caught."

Beth laughed softly against Sam's throat—teeth grazing the pulse point. "Then be quiet."

She kissed her—slow at first, testing.

Sam resisted for half a second—stiff, conflicted, then kissed her back.

Tongues met. Teeth grazed. Beth's hands slid down Sam's sides, thumbs dragging along her graceful nakedness.

Beth broke the kiss and turned her so Sam's back was against the wall tile. Water spilled over them both, muffling sound, turning the world small and private. Beth slid her dribbled her fingers down Sam's pelvis, teasing them over Sam's vulva, plump as an olive.

Beth looked up, letting residual water drip from her lashes—and spread Sam's legs with gentle pressure.

"Beth—please—"

Beth didn't make her beg long. She leaned in, tongue working overtime with aggressiveness and dominance.

Beth worked her with focus—fingers sliding deeper, her other hand sliding up to cup Sam's breast, nipple not forgotten. She added two fingers—slow, curling inside, pressing against her sweet spot, making Sam's thighs tremble. Sam's hips rocked—small, helpless jerks—chasing the pressure.

"Look at me," Beth murmured, pulling back just enough to speak.

Sam's eyes snapped open—glassy, desperate. She stared deep into Beth's soul.

Sam tensed up, back arching, a low, broken cry. Her thighs clamped, her hips bucked. A wave rolled through her—somehow violent and calm at the same time. Beth didn't stop—kept ripping into her, just softly enough to keep her path, and harsh enough to make it count.

She drew more aftershocks out one at a time, until Sam couldn't help but collapse.

Beth guided her down to the floor.

Sam moaned into her mouth, hands roaming, shoving at Beth with savory pleasure. "How are you so good?"

Sam, still trembling, boneless, kissed her again—slow, sharing the taste of desire. They stayed pressed together under the spray, breathing hard, foreheads touching.

Sam arched over her, "You're trouble, trouble-maker."

They lay there, timeless.

The locker room was still empty, quiet except for the tinkling of the shower.

Chapter 29
A Familiar Face

The stadium lights blazed against the November night like four white suns, turning the field into a bright green island surrounded by black. Oakridge High's home side was packed. The playoff opener, against Northwood. The rivalry ran deep; banners from both sides clashed almost as much as the students did, red-and-gold versus navy-and-silver. Chants rose and fell in waves that crashed against the cold metal stands. The air smelled of hot chocolate, popcorn grease, wet turf, and the faint metallic bite of frost. Every breath fogged in the chill; every cheer sent plumes of white vapor into the sky.

The crowd was electric—parents in team parkas, students in face paint and letterman jackets, little kids bundled on laps waving foam fingers. The marching band hammered out fight songs between plays; the PA announcer's voice boomed over the speakers. The tension was palpable; this wasn't just a game. It was personal.

Beth hadn't even noticed who they were playing until the national anthem ended and the PA read the opponent roster. Northwood, her old school. The one she'd left in a hurry last spring after everything went sideways. She felt the first flicker of spite when Northwood took the field—same stupid uniforms, same stupid faces on the cheer squad. Her stomach twisted—hard. She knew she couldn't afford to be spotted.

The Oakridge cheer squad performed on the track—sharp, synchronized, crowd roaring approval—but Beth took every sneaky peek possible at the opposition bleachers, scanning for familiar faces, taking note of anyone she definitely needed to avoid.

Halftime was hectic. The stadium buzzed louder in the sudden lull—no plays, no whistles, just the raw pulse of thousands of people exhaling at once. The field cleared fast: Oakridge players jogged toward the locker room tunnel in a loose pack, shoulder pads clacking, cleats scraping turf. Northwood huddled on the far sideline, helmets off, heads bent around their coach like a prayer circle gone wrong. The marching band exploded into the fight song again—brass sharp, drums thundering.

The cheer squad was preparing for their halftime show, but Beth would miss it. She waited until they dispersed for water, then slipped off of the field, hoping she would blend in better at the concession stand, despite the uniform. She texted Benny to meet her behind the vending machines.

He appeared thirty seconds later—nervous, flushed from the cold, and something else. She didn't give him time to speak. She grabbed his hoodie strings, yanked him into the narrow gap between the machines and the chain-link fence.

"Did you miss me, Benny?" she whispered against his mouth, lips brushing his ear.

His eyes scolded her—wide, panicked. "My sister's right up there, Beth. We—"

She cut him off, kissing him harder—like he owed her tongue. Her lips were soft, tasted like cherry lip balm, with hints of salt and sweat. Every press sent tiny fireworks across his nerves—a mysterious mixture of femininity and shamelessness that made his head spin.

He groaned low in his throat, hands coming up instinctively to grip her hips through her cheer shorts.

She took him by the wrist, "Come on, Benny, be a man, grab my ass."

"Beth—we, can't—do this—here," he gasped between each kiss.

Finally, she let him breathe, voice rough and cracking, he said, "Someone's gonna see us."

"Relax, Benny," she murmured, sucking lightly at his neck, working her hands under his shirt, fingers dragging tingles across his abdomen. "No one's looking back here."

She pressed closer, knee sliding between his thighs, grinding just enough to make him grumble low in his chest. She mouthed at his neck, gripping her teeth to his skin with a vile anguish, sucking hard and thick on him. He was dazed in a drooling bliss, and already so hard that she could feel it through his jeans.

A sharp voice sliced through the air like a whip.

"What the actual fuck, Beth?"

They broke apart.

Lainey stood at the mouth of the narrow gap, arms crossed, face thunderous under the stadium lights.

Benny froze. "Lane..."

Lainey didn't look at him. Her eyes stayed locked on Beth—cold, furious, betrayed.

"You promised," she said, voice low and shaking. "You said you were trying to lay low. That you were done with the games. And instead you're… what? Fucking my brother behind the vending machines like some cheap cliché?"

Beth straightened slowly, wiping her mouth with the back of her hand. "Lainey, it's not like that."

"It's exactly like that, Beth!" Lainey stepped closer, boots crunching gravel. "You knew I was worried about him. You knew he isn't like you. And you still—"

She grabbed Benny's wrist, yanking him toward her. He stumbled, still dazed, lips swollen and shiny, neck already darkening with a fresh mark.

"We're leaving," Lainey snapped. "Now."

Benny shot Beth one last helpless look before Lainey dragged him through the fence.

"Good God," Lainey muttered furiously, towing him through the parking lot by the arm, "look at your neck! She marked you!"

Beth watched them disappear into the row of cars and turned to make her way back to the field as she heard the roars ramp up, covered by the sounds of the game as the third quarter began. She was mid-hurry, back to the squad, when she locked eyes with a familiar face.

"Beth? Beth Harper?!" came chasing after her.

She turned quickly and kept walking, faster with every step.

Chapter 30
Beth's Ex

The final whistle shrieked. Oakridge 31, Northwood 28.

The scoreboard lights froze the numbers in electric blue, the crowd erupting in a roaring, stomping wave that shook the aluminum bleachers. Fireworks cracked overhead—red and gold sparks raining down like victory confetti—while the PA announcer bellowed the score one last time, voice hoarse from hours of calling plays.

Players on both sides met at midfield in the ritual handshakes, helmets off, shoulders slumped with exhaustion and adrenaline crash. Oakridge fans spilled onto the track. The air still smelled of popcorn, cut grass, and the faint burnt-sulfur tang of the fireworks.

The cheer squad gathered at the edge of the track—ponytails coming loose, makeup smudged from sweat and cold, voices raw from screaming. They huddled in a loose circle, trading exhausted high-fives and laughing about the pyramid that almost collapsed in the fourth quarter. Sam clapped once—sharp, captain-sharp—and jerked her head toward the parking lot.

The cheer squad walked off the field together—bag straps slung over shoulders, sneakers scuffing the asphalt path that curved past the ticket booth. Beth fell into step near the back, hood up, hands deep in her jacket pockets. She kept her head low—not dramatically, just enough.

She almost made it.

They were steps away from the parking lot, but someone waited against the chain link fence.

"Beth Harper."

She froze mid-step.

The squad, noticing what had just taken place, turned as one.

She stood there like she had no escape. He looked just as familiar as ever—tall, broad-shouldered, thick dark hair. Still wearing his Northwood Baseball jacket with the silver 7 stitched on the sleeve.

"Who's this?" Jenna asked, eyebrow arched.

Beth exhaled through her nose. "He's nobody. Keep walking. I'll catch up."

Debbie snorted. "Nobody? He looks like he's about to cry, or propose."

Kayla smirked. "Or both."

Beth's voice dropped—low, sharp, no room for argument. "Walk."

The girls exchanged glances—half amused, half annoyed—but Sam gave a small nod and jerked her chin toward the lot. "Five minutes, Beth. Don't make us come back for you."

They moved on, voices fluttered with whispers and gossip.

"Beth Harper"

He stepped closer—slow, like he wasn't sure she'd bolt.

"Johnny Carver..." she sighed.

"Didn't think I'd ever see you again," he said.

"Didn't think I'd see you either," she replied, arms crossed tight over her chest.

He studied her—eyes flicking over the cheer skirt, the hoodie, the way she held herself like she was ready to run or fight. "You look... different."

Beth tilted her head. "New school. New squad. New me."

Johnny nodded slowly. "I doubt that."

Her jaw tightened. "I'm leaving, Johnny."

"Yeah." He rubbed the back of his neck. "You know, I know where you go to school now, and well, people talk."

Beth's angry forced grin thinned. "Yeah, Johnny, they do."

He stepped closer—close enough she could smell his familiar cologne.

"What do you want from me, Johnny?"

He reached out—hesitant—brushed a loose strand of hair from her cheek. "I missed you, you know. After you left. It wasn't the same."

Beth caught his wrist before his fingers could linger. "Don't."

"I'm not your girl anymore."

Silence stretched—cold air biting at her exposed neck, distant cheers still echoing from the parking lot.

He shoved his hands in his pockets. "You coming back for the rematch next week?"

"Not if you're here."

Johnny gave her a small, crooked smile—the same one that used to make her weak. "Better give me what I want now then."

Beth's mouth twitched. "Johnny, I swear..."

"Oh, Beth, have you really gotten so naive?"

"Fine, but then we're through, and so are the rumors."

She looked back through the parking lot.

The squad was all leaning against the bus—arms crossed, eyebrows raised, watching.

"I'm gonna walk home!" she yelled to them.

🌂

They walked in silence to the far corner of the visitor parking lot where Johnny's black Jeep sat under the dim shadows of a large tree casting shadows from the flickering sodium lamp that towered over it. The rest of the Northwood fans had mostly cleared out; only a few stragglers were still loading coolers and folding chairs into trunks. The stadium lights were being shut down section by section, quickly plunging the area into darkness. Beth kept her hood up, hands shoved deep in her pockets, breath fogging in short, sharp bursts.

Johnny unlocked the doors with a chirp. "Get in."

She climbed into the passenger seat without a word. He started the engine but didn't drive—just let the heater blow lukewarm air while the dashboard lights painted their faces green. The radio stayed off. The only sound was the low rumble of the motor and the occasional distant car horn.

Johnny turned to her first.

He didn't speak. He just leaned across the console, one hand cupping the back of her neck, and kissed her neck—smelling faintly of Gatorade and mint gum. Beth let him for half a second—lips parting on reflex—then jerked back.

"Stop."

He froze, hand still tangled in her hair. "What?"

She wiped her mouth with the back of her hand. "I said stop."

Beth stared straight ahead at the windshield.

Johnny shifted closer, crowding her against the door. His hand slid down to her thigh, squeezing through the thin cheer shorts. "Come on, Beth. Don't act like this."

She caught his wrist—firm, not gentle—and pushed his hand away. "I'm not acting."

He leaned in again, lips brushing her neck, trying to find the spot that used to make her melt. She turned her head sharply, shoulder pressing against the window. He pulled back just enough to look at her—really look. His expression darkened.

"At least pretend like you still like me, bitch."

The word landed like a dagger in her heart.

Beth's eyes snapped to his. "Excuse me?"

"You heard me." His voice dropping low and mean.

Beth's laugh was cold and hollow. "You act as if I owe you this."

Johnny's hand shot out—fast—grabbing her chin, forcing her to face him. "Fuck off, Beth. You know exactly what you owe me."

She didn't flinch. Just stared back—eyes flat, unreadable.

He searched her face for a long second, still holding her face with a grip that frightened her.

Beth didn't move.

He pulled himself over her—rough, impatient—her back pressing against the cracked leather seat. She didn't fight. Didn't help either. Just lay there as he shoved her shorts down and wrapped his fingers around the crotch of her underwear.

Beth sucked in a sharp breath. "Are you really going to—"

Johnny groaned a stark cry, withering out a broken, "Shut up. Shut up."

Beth's voice came out low, flat, timed to his thrusts.

"I'll—tell—them—all—your—dirty—se-crets—you—filthy—little—whore..."   he confessed, slamming his crotch against hers repeatedly, anchoring up with a few strokes, gripping her by the face, dragging it sideways.

She struggled an angry response through his grasp, spitting back with pressed cheeks, "Why don't you tell them how much you begged me for it last year. How you cried when I wouldn't give it up."

Johnny laughed—breathless, mean—his jeans scraping her legs as he worked the button loose.

Beth's nails dug into his shoulders—not to pull him closer, but to anchor herself. "You're—pa-thetic."

He grabbed her throat—not choking, just holding—thumb pressing under her jaw.

"Get off. Get off me, Johnny."

She quickly pulled her shorts back into place and pushed him away.

"It's like that? After everything you took from me?"

"That's probably the only thing I've ever been sorry about, Johnny. I know it's hard for you. I don't expect it to be easy, but you'll just have to learn to forgive me."

She fixed her hoodie zipper and swung the door open.

"Fucking bit—" the door slammed in his face.

Chapter 31

Maybe It Gets Better

The week ended with Beth feeling the pressure building fast—her secret was seeping out like ink in water, slow at first, then impossible to contain. She kept quiet all weekend, knowing what would await her at school. It was no secret that Johnny could spread rumors, but how would he do it?

By the time she walked into the school, she could feel the tension. Everyone was talking, and these whispers had teeth. In the girls' bathroom between classes, two sophomores at the sinks had gone quiet when she walked in. She overheard another group gossiping through an open classroom doorway. I heard she got locked up last year." A guy she didn't even know bumped shoulders with her in the hall and muttered, "Northwood says hi, Beth."

She smiled—tight, sharp—and kept walking, but the knot in her chest tightened with every step.

The championship series loomed like a storm cloud: Oakridge vs. Northwood rematch next Friday night. The entire school was already buzzing—pep rallies, posters everywhere, the marching band seemingly practicing endlessly.

Beth needed an excuse not to be at the game. A desperate one. She couldn't stand on the track in her uniform, cheering for Oakridge while Johnny spreads rumors on both sides. The truth waiting to blow up in her face in front of everybody—if she could even survive the week at this point.

☢

After practice, the squad lingered in the auxiliary gym—sweaty, laughing, peeling off tape and retying ponytails. Beth hung back near the mats, pretending to stretch longer than necessary, when Sam crooked a finger from the doorway.

"Outside. Now."

Beth followed her into the hallway.

The corridor was quiet.

Sam leaned against the cinderblock wall, arms crossed, eyes sharp.

"You got expelled?" Sam asked without preamble. "From Northwood?"

Beth froze for half a heartbeat. Then she exhaled through her nose. "Uh, yeah, what did you hear?"

Sam's eyebrows shot up. "Why the fuck did you lie? That's way cooler than 'I just moved here.'"

Beth shrugged one shoulder. "Didn't want the drama."

Sam studied her—long, assessing. "Bullshit. What are you really hiding?"

Beth met her gaze. "Nothing you need to worry about."

Sam pushed off the wall, stepping closer. "You're on my squad. If it's gonna blow up in our faces—especially right before playoffs—I need to know."

Beth's mouth curved—just the corner. "It won't."

Sam didn't look convinced. "You sure? Because Patty's already sniffing around. She cornered me in the hall today, asking if I knew anything. She's got that look—like she's about to start digging."

"Let her dig," Beth suggested, "she'll get bored."

Sam exhaled hard. "You're playing with fucking fire, Beth."

Beth stepped closer—close enough that their bare arms brushed. "I like fire."

Sam's eyes flicked at her. "If you're going to burn, bitch, we're not going down with you."

Beth frowned at her, tilting her head. "Girl... Promise."

Sam shook her head, but there was a glimpse of flickering admiration in her eyes. "Get your ass back inside. We've got conditioning tomorrow at 6 a.m. Don't be late."

Beth nodded once and slipped back into the gym.

Chapter 32
Snake & Apple

B eth had always been good at reading rooms—except, apparently, this one.

The banter between her and Mr. Johnson had always been harmless, or so she'd thought: her complaining about students, him complaining about parents. But in her head, replaying it later, it twisted into something charged, flirtatious. An opening. A chance to finally turn the quiet tension she'd imagined between them into reality.

The other teachers already whispered about how he looked at her. Why not lean into it?

She waited until the building was mostly empty after school, the hallways dim and echoing. Mr. Johnson was still in his classroom, grading papers under the harsh fluorescent light. Beth knocked softly, then stepped in without waiting for an answer, closing the door behind her.

"Sir," she said, voice trembling just enough to sell it. "Mr... I... Can I talk to you?"

He looked up, surprised, setting his pen down. "Beth? Everything okay?"

She didn't answer right away. Instead, she crossed the room, eyes already glassy, and let her shoulders shake. The tears came easily—she'd practiced in the mirror plenty of times before for countless reasons. One sob, then another, until she was crumbling right in front of him.

He stood immediately, concern etching his face. "Hey, whoa—what happened?"

She stepped closer, letting him pull her into a comforting hug. His arms were solid, hesitant at first, then firmer as she pressed against him. She buried her face in his shoulder, inhaling the faint scent of his cologne mixed with chalk dust.

"I thought... I thought you felt it too," she whispered brokenly. "The way we talk, the looks in class... I misread everything, didn't I? I'm such an idiot."

"Beth, I—" He tried to pull back to look at her, but she clung tighter, turning her face up in a way so that he saw her more as a mess of puckered lips and wet eyes than anything else.

"Nobody likes me—I'm just the horrible new girl—you're my only friend..."

Before he could protest, she shifted—with a hanging, quick whip of her body—she pushed him gently back until he sat on the edge of his desk. In one fluid motion, she straddled his lap, knees bracketing his hips, her skirt riding up just enough to make the position unmistakable.

His hands froze on her waist. "Beth, wait—this isn't—"

"Shhh," she murmured, rocking subtly against him, feeling him stiffen beneath her—whether from shock or interest, she didn't care. "I've been so bad, I can't be throwing myself at you like this... I deserve to be punished."

His breathing stopped for a moment. She could see the war in his eyes: teacher caution, professional lines, versus the heat building where their bodies met.

"Is this why you got—"

"Come on," she whispered, guiding one of his hands lower, to the curve of her ass. "Spank me. I've been a *very* bad girl."

He hesitated, fingers flexing against her. Then—slowly, experimentally—he lifted his hand and brought it down in a firm smack. The sound cracked through the quiet room. Beth gasped, arching into it, her nails digging into his arms.

"Harder," she begged. "Please. Mark me. Make sure no one else knows... but you'll know."

Another smack, then another, each one pulling a moan from her throat. His control frayed visibly—his free hand slid up her back, into her hair. Her head fell back, exposing her neck.

"Yes—yes!" she hissed." Harder... Harder!"

He continued to smack. She continued to beg.

"Oh, yes! I am yours! Spank me!"

His face fell into her neck.

"Leave a mark there too."

She felt his mouth open, hot and moist, sucking hard against the sensitive skin just below her ear. The pull was sharp, deliberate, the kind of mark that would bloom dark purple by morning.

He continued to spank her, harder each time, losing himself more with each stroke and each suck.

"Yes—yes! Harder—I'm yours! Leave your mark—Yes!"

Beth whimpered, grinding down harder as he bit gently, then soothed with his tongue. "Yes... just like that. That's so fucking hot. I'm your bad girl."

His breathing was ragged now, the last of his resistance crumbling. One hand stayed on her hip, guiding her movements, while the other delivered another sharp spank that made her cry out softly.

When he finally pulled back to look at the darkening hickey, his eyes were dark with something possessive. "This... this stays between us."

Chapter 33
Boiled Frog

She kept the whole school on a short leash while the rumor mill spiral around her again—tugging at Benny's heart strings with every passing glance, slipping notes into Alex's locker with filthy promises, openly flirting with guys she had never even met, and most of all treading out rumors about girls like Patty and Lainey; though it was doubtful anyone would actually believe her. She even hung a threat of accusation over Mr. Johnson for a while because it made her eyes roll with orgasmic pleasure at just the simple thought of all the power she held over him.

"Heard you got expelled from Northwood," Patty said as she cornered her at her locker, voice syrupy-sweet. "Or was that just a rumor? Well, whatever it is, I'm going to find out. I'm sure by now you've noticed that I'm well on track to be elected Prom Queen this year. I trust you won't try to tamper with that in any way, given that I might actually have to use it against you."

Beth walked away carelessly with a swindling saunter—hips swaying, ponytail bouncing—leaving Patty staring after her, jaw clenched.

The entire school was already in playoff fever—hallways papered with red-and-gold posters, PA announcements hyping the rematch, teachers letting classes devolve into game talk. Beth walked the halls feeling every eye on her—some curious, some hostile, some seemingly almost all-knowing. The Northwood rumors had taken root: "Wasn't she the one who got locked up?"

"I heard she slept with half the football team."
"Who's that Johnny guy? He seemed pissed."

She kept her head down, hood up when she could, smiling through it all.

At lunch she sat with the squad—laughing at Jenna's jokes, stealing fries from Kayla's tray, letting Sam's knee brush hers under the table—but her mind was elsewhere.

The rematch was on Friday. She needed an out. Fast.

By last period, she'd decided: fake illness. The flu, something contagious enough to keep her home without question. She'd call Sam Thursday night, cough dramatically over the phone if she had to. The squad would be pissed, but they'd survive without her for one game.

She could handle the fallout later.

The squad was changing in the locker room, forcing Beth to strip down.

Debbie noticed it first. She reached out and poked the dark mark on Beth's neck—now a swollen violet shadow the shape of someone's open mouth. "Hey girl, who's the mystery mouth?"

Beth shrugged, dropping smoothly into a deep lunge stretch on the mat, one leg extended long behind her. "Wouldn't you like to know."

The squad was scattered around the auxiliary gym floor—half of them sitting cross-legged, peeling off ankle tape, the other half lying on their backs staring at the ceiling fan while they caught their breath. The air smelled of sweat, rubber mats, and the faint chemical tang of the floor cleaner the janitors used after hours. Someone's phone was still playing the last thirty seconds of their practice playlist—low bass thumping against the cinderblock walls.

Jenna snorted from her spot on the floor. "She's never gonna tell. Probably because it's embarrassing. Like, really embarrassing."

Kayla grinned, twisting her water bottle cap back on. "Or it's someone we'd roast her for. Like the kid who helps in the cafeteria."

Sarah propped herself on her elbows. "Or that Benny kid. I'm still not convinced it's not that Benny kid."

The group dissolved into laughter—easy, tired, the kind that comes after a long practice when everyone's too spent to really mean the teasing.

Beth just smiled—small, private, unbothered—and switched legs, keeping her eyes on the stretch.

Sam, who'd been wiping her face with the hem of her tank, finally spoke. She didn't look up from the towel she was folding.

"Are you going to tell us why you got kicked out?"

The laughter died instantly.

Beth stopped mid-stretch, back perfectly straight, ponytail hanging like a rope down her spine. Then she finished the motion, rolling forward into a forward fold so her forehead touched her knee, her face hidden for a second.

The gym went completely quiet.

Beth exhaled slowly through her nose, then sat up—graceful, controlled—and met Sam's eyes across the mat.

"You mean Northwood," she said. Not a question.

Sam didn't blink. "Yeah. I mean Northwood."

Beth tucked a loose strand of hair behind her ear. "It's not that interesting."

Sam tilted her head. "Try me."

Beth glanced around, a quick sweep of the other girls. Jenna had sat up, arms wrapped around her knees, openly listening. Debbie's eyebrows were halfway to her hairline. Kayla had stopped drinking water. Sarah and Riley exchanged a look but didn't speak.

Beth let out a small, dry laugh. "Fine. I got expelled. Happy?"

A ripple of surprise moved through the group—eyes widening, mouths parting slightly.

Sam leaned back on her hands. "For what?"

Beth shrugged one shoulder. "Fighting. Mostly."

"Mostly?" Jenna echoed, voice rising half an octave.

Beth's mouth curved—just the tiniest smirk. "There was a guy. Football player. Quarterback. Thought he ruled the school. I dated his brother and..."

They all spoke in shock and unison, "And?"

Silence again.

She got up and walked out, Sam chasing after her.

The hallway was a ghost town.

Beth stormed through them, mind racing, she was desperate for an exit.

Her sneakers skid on the polished tile, ponytail coming loose, breath sharp, wet gasps. She didn't look back. Didn't need to. She could feel the weight falling in over her head; the weight of Johnny's ghost, the weight of Lainey's stare, Patty's threat, Sam's suspicion. It pressed against her ribs until she couldn't breathe. She shoved into the nearest bathroom to catch a breather.

Inside: empty stalls, chipped sinks, the faint smell of bleach and old perfume. One fluorescent tube flickered. Beth staggered to the last sink, gripped the porcelain edge so hard her knuckles went white, and let the tears come.

Not quite crying. Ugly sobs, just the ones she couldn't hold in. Her shoulders shaking, mascara streaking, chest heaving like she was drowning. She stared at her reflection—red eyes, swollen lips, the faded violet mark on her neck mocking her—and hated everything she saw.

The door banged open behind her.

Footsteps—quick, purposeful.

"Beth."

Sam's voice—low, steady, not angry.

Beth didn't turn. She just kept crying, harder now, like the sound of Sam's boots on tile had broken whatever dam was left.

Sam didn't hesitate. She walked straight up, grabbed Beth's shoulders—firm but not rough—and turned her around.

Beth tried to twist away, but Sam held on.

"Look at me."

Beth shook her head, tears dripping onto the tile.

Sam cupped her face—gentle, thumbs wiping under her eyes. "Hey. Hey. Breathe."

Beth sucked in a ragged breath, then another. The sobs slowed to hiccups.

Sam didn't let go. "Talk."

Beth's voice came out small, wrecked. "It's too much..."

Sam waited.

"It's all too much, they're all talking, and they know nothing."

Sam's thumbs stilled on her cheeks.

Beth's eyes flicked up—red-rimmed, glassy. "I can't do this anymore. I can't keep pretending I'm fine. I'm not fine. I'm fucking terrified."

She broke again—fresh tears spilling, body shaking. She folded forward until her forehead rested against Sam's shoulder, hands clutching the front of Sam's hoodie like it was the only thing keeping her upright.

Sam didn't pull away.

She wrapped her arms around Beth—slow, careful—then tighter. One hand stroked down Beth's back in long, soothing lines. The other cradled the back of her head, fingers threading through her hair.

"I've got you," Sam murmured against her temple. "You're not alone in this."

Beth clung harder, face buried in Sam's neck. "I lied to you. About Northwood. About why I left. About... everything."

Sam didn't flinch. "I know."

"And you're still here?"

Sam looked deeply at her. "Yeah. I'm still here."

Beth's jumbled through her cries. "But, why?"

"Because, Beth, you can trust me," Sam said simply.

Beth gimped through a few more sobs, "I—can't—tell—you."

"Why can't you tell me, Beth?"

"You—wouldn't—understand."

"Try me... Come on, Beth. No more hiding. Just you and me, right here."

Beth stared at her—chest rising and falling, mascara streaked, lips trembling.

Then she nodded.

"Okay," she whispered. "Okay."

She leaned forward again—not for comfort this time, but for something else. Her forehead rested against Sam's, noses brushing, breaths mingling.

"I'm scared," Beth admitted, voice barely audible. "I thought if I controlled everything—if I played everyone right—no one could hurt me. But, John, he…"

Sam's hand slid to cup the back of Beth's neck—warm, steady. "What happened?"

She was hyperventilating now, making less sense with every breath, her mind flooded. "I—he…"

Sam leaned in—slow, deliberate—and kissed her. A promise pressed against her lips.

Beth melted into it—hands sliding up Sam's arms, gripping her shoulders like she was afraid to fall.

When they broke apart, Beth's breathing was steadier. The tears had slowed.

Sam rested her forehead against Beth's again. "It's okay, I'm here for you."

Beth swallowed. "I—he—because I, he, and t hen..."

Sam's thumb traced her jaw, thumbing at the divot of her cheek. "Beth?"

Her face had gone pale.

"Beth?"

Beth fainted.

Chapter 34

A Change of Heart

Beth woke to the steady beep of a heart monitor and the sharp, antiseptic smell of hospital linoleum.

Her eyelids felt glued shut; when she finally pried them open, the room swam into focus in pieces: pale blue curtains, an IV stand dripping clear fluid into her left arm, a small window showing a gray winter sky. The fluorescent light overhead was dimmed, but it still buzzed faintly. Her head throbbed in dull waves—dehydration, exhaustion, maybe a sedative they'd given her in the ER. She remembered fragments: running through the hall, crying in the bathroom, Sam holding her, chest tightening, vision tunneling, knees buckling, then nothing.

She looked around, eyes still blurry.

"Hey, sunshine, you're awake," a voice bounced around in distant echoes like it was underwater.

It was Sam.

Beth sat up a bit to see her, "Hey, girl."

"Glad to see you're awake," Sam said. "The school tried to call your mom, but she didn't pick up. Does she have a work number?"

"It's okay, she doesn't need to know."

"Well, you can explain that one to the nurse. How are you feeling?"

"I feel fine. I fainted?"

"Yeah, you had a panic attack over something. They want to keep you overnight."

"Oh, that's fine, I guess."

"Beth, this seems pretty serious, something to panic about. Are you going to tell me what you're so worried about? You said something about that Johnny guy?"

"Sam," she stuttered, "I can't.

"Fine. Fine. I'm going to go get the girls; they want to see you."

Sam brought in the cheer squad—quiet, subdued, none of their usual chaos. Jenna first, eyes red-rimmed. Debbie carrying a small stuffed bear with a red-and-gold ribbon. Kayla holding a bouquet of cheap grocery-store carnations. Sarah and Riley were hovering near the foot of the bed. Sam brought up the rear, arms crossed, expression unreadable.

They gathered around—awkward, careful, like they weren't sure if she'd break again if they got too close.

Jenna spoke first, voice thick. "You look like you're doing better."

Beth tried to smile. It felt like cracking concrete. "Sorry. Didn't mean to scare you all."

Debbie set the bear on the blanket. "Shut up. We're just glad you're okay."

Kayla placed the flowers on the side table. "The doctor said panic attack. Like, bad one. You've been holding it together too long."

Sarah nodded. "We should've noticed."

Riley added quietly, "We're sorry we didn't."

Beth's throat closed. She looked away—toward the window, toward the IV pole, anywhere but their faces. "It's not your fault."

Long after Sam and the girls left, Benny showed up.

His hoodie was zipped to his chin, hiding the marks Beth had left.

Beth sat up a little straighter, IV line tugging. "Hey. Wasn't expecting you."

"Oh yeah, I heard, you know, those cheer girls can't keep their mouths shut.

Beth nodded. "Yeah. You got that right. Does Lainey know you're here?"

"Yeah, actually, she's wishing you well."

"That sure sounds like her."

Benny looked at her—really looked. "Anything I should know about?"

Beth's mouth twitched. "Yeah, let me be honest, you should keep your distance, I'm a disaster."

Benny laughed. "Yeah, but you know I'm not going to do that."

Beth glanced at Benny. He looked miserable—eyes red, shoulders hunched.

"Come on, Benny, don't be so naive, you know I was only playing you for a fool."

Benny stared at her for a while, and when he finally spoke again, his voice was broken. "Yeah, Lainey warned me. But you're irresistible."

She smiled at him—small, real. "Let's just be friends, Benny. Nobody has to get hurt."

"Beth—" he stopped in thought for a few moments. "Promise?"

He sat with her for a while, mainly in silence, some small talk, mostly jokes about people at school.

She closed her eyes for a while, and Benny decided to let her sleep.

As he left the room, he bumped shoulders with Alex. The broad force spun Benny around enough to taunt him. He filled with jealousy as he looked back at him, but ultimately he had to let it go and went home.

Alex's monstrous shadow looming over her woke her up.

"Oh, were you sleeping?"

"Ummm... You? You're here?"

"Yeah, why not? You said it yourself, no strings attached. What, you think I have no heart?"

She blinked at him in a quick thought, "No, I—"

"I brought chocolates, you like chocolates, right?

"Everyone likes chocolates, Alex."

"That's true, I almost got you flowers, but chocolates are better, you can't eat flowers."

"Good point."

"Who's the kid?"

"Huh?—Oh, you mean Ben? Just a friend."

Alex laughed. "You don't have friends." A witty, cutting joke.

"We're not friends?" she queried with a wink.

"Hmmm, maybe, are you going to change your ways?" he asked.

"No, Alex, probably not."

"Fine, Beth, but you have to play nice with me."

"Deal."

"Hey, you're going to be alright, yeah? Call me if you need a ride home."

Chapter 35

Spring Break Madness

S he had successfully avoided the rivalry game; Sam would let her off to dodge the drama, but the rumors, she couldn't help with that much. To her surprise, rumors around the school had shifted to more about the panic attack and her fainting than anything else. Still, she didn't know what they did and didn't actually know. A few weeks passed, and soon, the only thing on everyone's mind was spring break. Of course, Beth was back to her old ways, but now her target pool thinned, and her actions were more calculated. She had ample time to plan her next move in the shadows while everyone's eyes were diverted to the blooming adventure of spring.

Spring break hit like a long, lazy exhale after the suffocating pressure of playoffs and rumors. The school was empty—lockers silent, hallways dim, the usual buzz now null. Beth's mind was peaking with ideas for her week of freedom. It was only the first night, and she was already bored.

Bone-deep, skin-crawling bored.

She scrolled through her messages—Sam's text from last night, Benny's from last week, and a couple of squad group-chat messages she hadn't opened. Nothing urgent. Nothing interesting.

She opened Benny's thread instead.

What are you doing for spring break?

She hit send, then flopped back against the pillows, staring at the ceiling fan spinning slow circles.

His reply came in under two minutes.

Nothing really.

Lainey's at some debate camp thing.

Getting ready for bed.

You?

Bored. Come pick me up.

Now?

Yeah. Now.

A pause—three dots blinking, disappearing, blinking again.

I can sneak out after my parents go to sleep.

Be there in 20.

Beth grinned—small, sharp—and rolled out of bed.

She dressed fast: black leggings, cropped hoodie (red and gold, squad colors), simple sneakers. Hair in a messy bun. A bit of mascara, easy on the lip gloss. She looked in the mirror—the fire was back in her eyes. Good.

She was just finishing up her makeup when she thought she heard Benny pull up outside. She caught his eye as she walked to the truck. He looked nervous but excited—hoodie up, windows down, music low.

Beth climbed into the passenger seat, leaned over the console, and kissed him quick—teeth grazing his bottom lip.

He was eager. "What do you want to do?"

She laughed. "Don't ask questions, just drive... Let's pick up the girls. I'll call Sam."

First stop, Sam's house. A lot of the girls were still there from their meetup earlier, and the rest of them they grabbed along the way. One by one, they piled into the bed of his truck.

"I knew you hung out with this kid," Sam said through the back window.

"He's a good boy," Beth joked.

"Seems that way," Riley said.

"Wow, that's a lot of pretty girls," Benny said, looking into his rear-mirror.

"Aren't you lucky?" Kayla joked.

"Where next?" he asked.

"Grocery store, please," Beth commanded.

"What you got in mind?" Jenna asked

"You'll see."

The girls looked at each other, puzzled.

The truck rolled into the grocery store lot just after dark. The neon **OPEN** sign flickered above the automatic doors, casting a sickly green glow across the mostly empty parking spaces. Benny killed the engine and looked over at Beth in the passenger seat—cheeks still flushed from the wind and laughter, hoodie zipper half-down, eyes bright with the same reckless energy that had kept his interest in her.

Beth grinned—sharp, mischievous—and hopped out before he'd even unbuckled. "Come on. Quick in, quick out."

The squad piled out of the bed—Jenna, Debbie, Kayla, Sarah, Riley, and Sam. They moved like a pack of caffeinated wolves: hoods up, sneakers scuffing, voices hushed but giddy. Beth stopped at the front, calling out orders like an army sergeant, "You girls go get as much toilet paper as you can carry. Benny, come with me to the egg isle."

Inside the store, the fluorescent lights were too bright, the air too cold, and the atmosphere too quiet. A single cashier, early twenties, bored, looked up from his phone behind the register. His eyes tracked the group as they fanned out down the aisles: six girls in hoodies and leggings, one nervous-looking guy trailing behind them like he'd been kidnapped. Based on the way the girls moved, he half-way almost thought he could be their next victim too.

The gang met up at the front of the store, loaded now with six mega-roll packs and an almost countless stack of egg cartons, looking increasingly like they were ready for war.

"Is everyone here?" Beth asked.

The cashier watched them come forward with all their ammunition. He was knowingly observant; six teenage girls plus one twitchy guy, nothing but toilet paper and eggs, during spring break? Classic.

His eyes scanned their faces. "Bake sale or a riot?"

Jenna snorted. Debbie elbowed her.

Benny shifted uncomfortably. "Just... pranking some friends."

The guy looked straight at Beth.

"As long as you don't get my house," he said, half-joking, half-serious. His tone made it clear he knew exactly what they were up to.

Beth met his eyes—steady, unflinching—and smiled wider.

"No promises," she said lightly.

"Total's $93.42."

Benny fumbled for his wallet; the girls all turned to look at Sam.

Sam shrugged and then gave him a $100 bill. "Keep the change," she said.

Back at the truck, the girls piled the supplies into the bed—TP rolls wedged between the wheel wells, egg cartons stacked like crates of ammo.

Benny climbed into the driver's seat, hands on the wheel, still looking shell-shocked.

Beth slid in beside him, leaned over the console, and kissed his cheek.

He exhaled—shaky, half-laughing. "I'm gonna have a heart attack."

She grinned. "Not yet. Night's still young."

Sam climbed into the bed with the others, banging on the roof once.

"Let's roll!"

The truck pulled out of the lot—headlights sweeping the empty street, tires humming, the bed full of giggling girls and enough supplies to paper half the neighborhood.

They started small—some junior's house talked shit about the cheer squad. Benny slowed to a smooth roll, coasting along the curb.

"That's the one!" Sam said.

They giggled like idiots—drive-by hyenas—long looped lobs of toilet paper, topped off by a few eggs.

Next house. Patty's house. Benny followed Sam's directions to perfection.

A long, tedious once over, Sam would have thrown all of it if she could.

Then they hit Mike's house—Patty's boyfriend.

"He lives right behind her," Sam yelled.

"Oh, how convenient," Beth said, rolling her eyes as she handed Sam an egg. "Special treatment?"

The night turned into chaos—controlled, gleeful chaos. The adrenaline kicked in. House after house caught stray eggs like friendly fire. Yolks splattering like yellow paint bombs. Toilet rolls flying like confetti. Tires squealing just enough to make the neighbors' porch lights flick on.

"One more stop."

"You're a menace," Benny said, looking over at Beth with a twinkle in his eye, smiling like he'd never smiled before.

Beth grinned back—wild, alive. "You love it."

Chapter 36

Oops...

B enny revved the engine—nervous, laughing—his foot hovering over the gas with compulsion. The truck sat idling at the curb around the corner from Johnny's house, headlights off, the bed full of giggling girls clutching the last of their TP rolls and egg cartons. The street was dead quiet—porch lights off, curtains drawn, only the occasional dog bark echoing from somewhere deeper in the neighborhood.

Beth leaned forward between the front seats, chin resting on Benny's shoulder, eyes locked on the dark two-story house at the end of the cul-de-sac. Johnny's Jeep was parked in the driveway—same black one she'd climbed out of after the stadium, same dented fender from last year's prank. The sight of it twisted something sharp in her chest—anger, lust, thrill, nostalgia, all tangled together.

"There," she said softly. "That's the one."

A ripple of awareness moved through the truck bed. Jenna leaned over the side rail. "Wait—your ex, Johnny?"

Beth's smile was thin. "The very one."

Kayla whistled low. "Oh, this is personal."

Debbie cracked her knuckles. "Say less."

Sarah handed her an egg. "We doing this or what?"

Beth looked at Benny.

"You in?" she asked him quietly.

He swallowed. Then nodded—slow, certain. "Yeah. I'm in."

Beth kissed his cheek—quick, grateful—then turned to the girls in the back.

"Let's light it up."

Benny eased the truck forward—slow, headlights off—until they were parallel with Johnny's front yard. The house was dark except for a single upstairs window glowing blue from a TV. Johnny was probably inside, thinking the night was over.

He had no idea.

Beth went first, leading the charge alone, Benny and the girls following her shortly after. She fired egg after egg, straight at his window, ecstatic with every smack, and every wet, yellow drip. The girls whooped—low, thrilled—admiring her bloodthirsty barrage. The girls just watched, sharing concerned glances.

Benny joined in.

He hurled eggs with surprising force. They rained down like hellfire meteorites—thick yolks exploding against the house, the mailbox, the porch steps—shell fragments littering the yard like spent bullet casings. TP rolls unfurled in long white streamers, draping across bushes, tangling in the low branches of the front-yard maple tree, and wrapping around the Jeep's side mirrors like mummy bandages. Sam filmed the whole thing on her phone, whispering commentary like a sports announcer.

The blue light upstairs flickered—someone moving.

A silhouette appeared at the window—Johnny, shirtless, staring down at the wreckage of his yard.

Beth lobbed a final egg that hit his window, splattering in front of his face with a satisfying crack.

Johnny's silhouette stiffened.

She met his eyes across the distance—through the dark, through the glass—and lifted her hand in a small, mocking wave.

Johnny's silhouette jerked—shoulders snapping straight, hand slapping the window frame in anger. She saw his mouth move; she could read the swears and curses from his lips so well that she could practically hear them.

Beth didn't wait for the encore.

She spun on her heel and ran.

Benny was already moving—half-stumbling backward, eyes wide with the same mix of terror and exhilaration that had him grinning like a fool. They sprinted across the lawn together—grass slick underfoot, low branches whipping at their faces, laughter bursting out of them in sharp, breathless bursts. Beth's sneakers skidded on wet leaves; Benny nearly tripped over a garden gnome but caught himself, grabbing her wrist to keep them both upright.

They zigzagged toward the curb, dodging large rocks and bushes like spies sneaking through a laser security maze in a heist movie. Beth vaulted the low brick wall like it was a stunt ramp, ponytail whipping around behind her. Benny dove for the driver's side door, nearly sliding across the hood of his truck like a baseball player stealing home. He yanked the door open so hard it bounced on its hinges. He jumped inside and slammed the door shut so fast he damn near caught his foot in it. Beth fumbled into the passenger seat. Benny threw himself behind the wheel, key trembling in his shaky hands, the engine stuttering as he over-turned it in a panic.

The girls in the bed went silent for half a second.

The engine roared to life—the girls erupted in cheer.

Beth twisted in her seat, turning toward "Floor it!"

Benny didn't need to be told twice. He stomped the gas.

The truck peeled out—splattering eggs still echoing off the walls, rolls thumping into the trees, tires chirping, girls screaming; like it couldn't be more obvious.

Beth looked back at the girls, breathing hard, adrenaline singing through her veins, the wind whipping through her hair. She smiled at them with a sharp satisfaction.

She faced forward, turned her attention to the passing streetlights, and stared out the windshield with a loss in her eyes.

Benny glanced at her—half-awed, half-terrified.

Beth slumped down in her seat, a deep, unsettling feeling rushed across her. "I think I just made a huge mistake."

Chapter 37
Prom Night

Things were oddly calm for weeks. Beth kept her head down, her smiles polite but distant, and no one pushed. The school's attention had shifted entirely to prom—dress fittings, ticket sales, and after-party plans. Beth became background noise, a ghost in the hallways, while the senior class buzzed with sequins and anticipation.

Prom night arrived in a haze of perfume, rented tuxedos, and music everywhere it didn't belong. The cheer squad piled into the stretch limo, all glitter and laughter, heels clicking against the bar as they passed around flasks. Sam sat across from Beth, arms folded, watching her like a hawk. She'd been waiting for the other shoe to drop; the rumor mill had been too quiet for too long. Beth looked flawless—crimson dress hugging every curve, hair swept up, matching her sparkling golden mascara. Her lips painted a perfect light pink, pressed together like keeping quiet was too much, ready to burst open with drama at any moment. Her eye-shadow matching her bright blue eyes, both hiding secrets and making them known with a daring statement.

Sam knew better than to trust the calm. Halfway through the night, the squad ditched their dates with practiced ease. "Girls' night," leaving the boys alone to argue over who was buying the next round of mocktails. They claimed a corner booth in the dimly lit lounge attached to the venue, music thumping through the walls. Beth's eyes kept drifting—scanning, calculating—until they locked on Mike.

Patty's boyfriend. Tall, easy smile, proudly sporting his tennis jacket and casual slacks like he couldn't care less to dress nicely for the event. He was laughing at something one of the guys said, oblivious.

Beth waited. Patient. When Patty excused herself to the bathroom—touching up lipstick, probably—Beth rose smoothly, glass in hand, and crossed the room like she owned it.

She slid into the seat beside Mike without asking.

"Mike, right? I'm Beth. I don't think we've met."

Mike turned, eyebrows lifting in mild surprise, then recognition. He leaned back, amused. "I know who you are."

"Of course you do," she said, voice low, teasing.

"What do you want?"

Beth smiled, slow and deliberate. "I just wanted to say hello." She let her knee brush his under the table, "Did Patty mention how much fun I can be?"

His gaze flicked down to her lips, then back up.

She leaned closer, breath warm against his ear. "Fitting in comes in many forms," she murmured. "And I'm very good at making people feel... included."

Mike's eyes held a depth of understanding—maybe guilt, maybe curiosity, maybe both. He didn't speak for a long beat. Then he stood, offering his hand.

They slipped out a service door into the cool night air, the bass fading behind them like a heartbeat slowing to nothing. Beth led him around the side of the building to a shadowed alcove between the dumpsters—private enough, reckless enough. The smell of spilled beer and warm asphalt hung thick in the air like some group of seniors was secretly pre-gaming there earlier. She took his pants down in hurried pulls, fingers deft and impatient. He spun her around and pushed her against the wall, quick to hike up her dress and yank her panties aside with a rough tug that made her let out a purr-like gasp.

He set a brutal pace. Skin slapped skin in sharp, rhythmic echoes off the brick. Obscene thoughts flashed through her mind—dirty, possessive, vengeful. Every thrust drove a sharp gasp out of her, her palms sprawling against the rough brick for balance, nails scraping as she arched back into him. She bit her lip hard enough to taste copper, trying to stifle the sounds, but they escaped anyway—raw, triumphant little moans that mingled with his low grunts. Her hips rolled to meet him, greedy, chasing the edge. Sweat slicked the small of her back where her dress bunched; his fingers dug into her waist like he was anchoring himself to the moment, to her, to the wrongness of it all. She tilted her head back, throat exposed, letting one hand slide down to touch herself—fingers circling fast, matching his rhythm until her thighs trembled and her gasps turned jagged.

They didn't even hear the door open.

Mia stood frozen in the doorway, phone light still on from checking the time. Her face drained of color, then flushed hot with a mix of shock and secondhand embarrassment for them both. The clutch in her hand slipped from numb fingers and hit the ground with a clatter that cut through the haze.

Mike froze mid-thrust, buried deep, his breath ragged. Beth's eyes snapped open; she looked back over her shoulder, hair falling in disheveled strands across her face, and locked gazes with Mia. For a split second, something almost like amusement flickered in Beth's expression—caught, but not sorry.

Mia's voice cracked the silence like glass.

"You fucking whore."

Mike scrambled to pull away, yanking his pants up in frantic jerks, the zipper catching on fabric. "Mia, please—don't tell Patty."

"Oh, I am going to tell her, Mike." Mia's tone was ice, steady now, the initial shock hardening into something colder. "Not tonight. I'm not going to ruin prom for her—she deserves one night without this bullshit. But tomorrow? Or the next day? When she's smiling at you like you're still worth something? Yeah. I'm going to tell her. Sorry, not sorry."

Beth straightened slowly, smoothing her dress down with a strange, deliberate calm. Her chest still rose and fell, her posture still staggered and uneven. "You—know—what, Mia?" she sprang out—half slurred drunk speech, half breathless exhaustion.

"Go home, Beth, you're drunk," Mia spat out, her eyes shooting an expression that said the same thing.

Mia didn't wait for excuses or apologies. She bent, snatched her clutch from the pavement, and turned away in a quick mix of anger and disbelief. Her heels echoed like gunshots down the concrete corridor back toward the venue, each step deliberate, final.

The door clicked shut behind her.

Mike stood there panting, shirt half-tucked, face ashen. "Fuck. Fuck."

Beth adjusted the strap of her dress, wiped a smudge of lipstick from the corner of her mouth with her thumb, and glanced at him sidelong.

"Guess the night just got interesting," she said softly, almost sweetly.

She walked past him without another word, hips swaying, disappearing around the corner like nothing had even happened at all.

Chapter 38

Digging Up Her Past

Patty had driven the whole way to Northwood with her knuckles white on the steering wheel, radio off, mind racing: Mia wouldn't lie to her, of course, she expected Beth to stoop that low, she should have known. Mike's betrayal stuck lodged in her heart like shrapnel.

She needed answers, real ones, not the polished version Beth fed everyone at Oakridge. So she'd skipped last period, told the office she had a family thing, and crossed the county line to the rival school she'd only ever seen on game nights or in gossip threads.

Northwood High looked quieter than she'd expected on a weekday afternoon—fewer kids milling around, the parking lot half-empty. Patty parked near the visitor spots and stepped out, scanning faces like she was hunting ghosts. She asked a couple of freshmen near the flagpole if they knew Johnny; they shrugged and pointed vaguely toward the back fields. She tried the main office—closed for the day. A janitor sweeping the breezeway told her that there's a Johnny who always hung out at the baseball diamond after practice—that sounded like someone Beth would date to her.

She found him there alone, sitting on the bottom bleacher of the visitor side, elbows on knees, staring at the empty diamond like it owed him something. The Northwood jacket was slung over the seat beside him, sleeves inside-out, emblem facing up like a badge he couldn't quite shed. He didn't look up when her shadow fell across the dirt.

"Johnny?" Her voice came out softer than she'd planned—helpless, almost. She'd rehearsed sharp questions the whole drive, but standing there, the anger felt distant, replaced by something rawer.

He glanced sideways at her like he was trying to figure out if he knew her or not.

Patty took a tentative step closer, hands half-raised like she was approaching something skittish. "I... I drove here from Oakridge. I've been asking around. People said you might be out here. Can we talk about Beth Harper?"

Johnny let out a short, bitter laugh and looked away again. "Yeah? What about her?"

She sat on the bleacher a careful distance away, not too close. "From what I've heard, you're her ex, so I thought maybe you'd know why she got expelled. I need to know. The real story. Not the rumors, not whatever she's spinning at Oakridge."

He rubbed a hand over his face, shoulders tense. For a long moment, she thought he'd tell her to leave. Then the words came out low, clipped, like pulling teeth.

"She—She killed my brother. She lied about what really happened. Everyone believed her because she sold it so well. Cry on cue, play the victim. I lost friends, scholarship opportunities, everything. And she just... transferred. Clean break. Like it all never happened."

Patty's stomach twisted. She stared at the cracked clay of the infield, picturing Beth's easy smiles, the way she'd charmed the cheer squad from day one. "It's still a secret here, too, isn't it? To most people."

"Most," he said. "Some know pieces. Enough to avoid me. But the full thing? Nah. She made sure it stayed buried."

"That's terrible. If it counts for anything, I believe you."

"Thanks. What did she do to you?" he asked.

"Nothing as bad as that. Yet..."

"She will," he said. "She'll get to you."

Patty's hands clenched in her lap. Shock gave way to something colder, sharper. "And then she prances around school like she's not everyone's biggest problem. Like she can do whatever she wants. Like she's untouchable."

Johnny finally met her eyes. "She's not."

Patty nodded slowly, the helplessness from earlier hardening into resolve. "I'm not going to let her keep pretending anymore. Whatever it takes."

He studied her for a beat, then gave a small, grim nod. "Good. Make her feel it. Every damn bit."

Patty stood, brushing dirt from her jeans. She didn't say goodbye—just turned and walked back toward the parking lot, the promise settling heavier than before. Beth's secrets weren't staying buried anymore. Not if Patty had anything to say about it.

Chapter 39

Pretty Little Liar

A few days went by with no drama, but Beth was still hanging onto hesitation around every corner, fully expecting to have it out with Patty. The final bell had rung for the day. The hallways still buzzed with stragglers—lockers slamming, laughter echoing off the tile. Beth was alone at her locker, spinning the combination with one hand while texting with the other, when Patty appeared like a shadow sliding into frame.

Beth glanced up, a smile already forming out of habit. "Hey, Pats. You good?"

Patty didn't smile back. She planted herself square in front of the open locker door, arms crossed, blocking any easy exit. Her eyes were hard, unblinking.

"Beth—Harper," she said, voice low but carrying the weight of every syllable. "If that is your real name."

Beth's thumb froze over her phone screen. The smile faltered, then vanished. "What are you talking about?"

Patty leaned in closer, close enough that Beth could smell the faint mint of her gum. "You crossed the line for real this time. And guess what?" She paused, letting the silence stretch until it hurt. "I know your secret."

Beth's face went blank—pure deer-in-headlights—before she forced a laugh that sounded thin even to her own ears. "Okay, you're being weird. What secret? I don't have a—"

"Don't," Patty cut her off. "Don't play dumb. Not with me. Not after what you did at Northwood. I talked to your ex, Johnny. He still carries the scars you left on him. I know everything. His brother? You killed his brother, Beth. Poor guy."

Beth's hand tightened on the locker door until her knuckles whitened. Her voice dropped to a whisper. "You don't know what you're talking about."

"I know enough." Patty's gaze never wavered. "And I'm done pretending you're some innocent transfer. You think you can keep running from it? Hide behind that perfect smile? Nope... Not anymore."

Beth swallowed, eyes darting left and right like she was looking for an escape route. The hallway noise felt suddenly distant, muffled. "Patty, whatever you heard, it's not—"

"Save it." Patty stepped back just enough to give Beth room to breathe—but not enough to let her bolt. "I'm not here to listen to excuses. I'm here to tell you this: your free ride ends now. Every lie you told, every person you burned? It's coming back around. And I'm going to make sure you feel every inch of it."

Beth stared at her, chest rising and falling too fast. For the first time since she'd set foot in Oakridge, the mask cracked—just a hairline fracture, but Patty saw it.

Patty turned on her heel, voice carrying over her shoulder like a parting shot. "Watch your back, Beth Harper."

Chapter 40

Graduation Shenanigans

The graduation ceremony was already well underway under the bright May sun, the football field transformed into a sea of caps and gowns. Rows of folding chairs stretched across the turf, families fanning themselves with programs, the principal's voice droning through the PA system as names echoed one after another.

"Mike Halk."

A polite smattering of applause rose from the stands. Mike walked across the stage, shoulders squared, diploma in hand, forcing a smile that didn't reach his eyes. He glanced once toward the cheer section—Patty's spot—then looked away fast.

Next.

"Beth Harper."

The shift was immediate. A low murmur rippled through the crowd, then swelled. Boos started small—scattered along her classmates, hesitant—then built like a wave crashing over the field. Loud, unmistakable, rolling from almost every seat. Whistles, jeers, and a few shouted curses cut through the air. Beth's steps faltered for half a second on the stage stairs, but she lifted her chin, painted on that same flawless smile, and kept walking. The principal handed her the diploma with a tight, professional nod; she took it, turned to the crowd, and raised it like a trophy.

She descended the steps to a chorus of disapproval and walked right into the swell of boos, faces turned toward her like hissing snakes. The shame followed her all the way back to her seat.

Patty watched from her row, fists clenched in her lap, face burning. Mia had told her everything the morning after prom—every detail, no sugarcoating. Patty hadn't cried. She'd just gone quiet. Too quiet. She held it in for weeks, but seeing Beth up there soaking in the hate like it was applause, something inside her snapped.

The moment Beth sat down, Patty dove across two rows like a missile, tackling her from behind and knocking her off the chair. She was in a burning blackout rage, wrestling Beth around and striking her face over and over.

Beth retaliated with a sharp elbow to Patty's ribs.

Patty didn't slow down, pelting her with fists in almost instant succession.

They grappled, gowns tangling, caps knocked off, hair coming loose in furious handfuls. Patty yanked Beth's hair back.

"You!" she cried, voice cutting through the cheers and gasps like a blade.

Shouts erupted around them—"Fight! Fight!"—phones came out to record, and circles of bodies formed.

They grappled in a twisting fury, rolling across the grass, trading blows.

Beth wrestled her back, trying to defend herself, but Patty didn't let up. "My boyfriend? At prom? In a fucking alley like some cheap—"

Beth grabbed her by the hair and held her close to her body. "You're just mad because someone finally gave him what he wanted."

Patty's eyes flashed. She flipped Beth quick and hard, and mounted her. "You bitch. You ruined everything for us. I hope it was worth it. I hope it was good!"

Beth let the moment linger, staring deep into her eyes, voice dropping to a venomous tone. "Oh, it was good. He fucked me stupid."

Patty's hand shot out, slapping her smooth and hard, her palm cracking across Beth's cheek with a sound that silenced the entire crowd. Beth's head snapped to the side.

"You're stupid, alright!" Patty snarled and then spat on her face, hard and good.

Beth recovered fast—too fast. She was midway stood and ready to fight, when security dragged them apart from each other.

Blood poured from Beth's nose, gown torn at the shoulder, hair wild, lipstick smeared across her chin like war paint. Patty held her bruised rib, kicking and screaming for more.

Meanwhile, the graduation continued—without them.

The principal's voice had cracked only once over the speakers—"Friends and family, we apologize for the interruption, please do not be concerned, the ceremony will proceed as scheduled."—then he powered through the rest of the names like nothing had happened. Caps sailed into the air on cue, cheers erupted in pockets, families snapped photos, and the band struck up a fight song one last time. But the energy felt off, brittle.

Whispers snaked through the rows of students:

—Did you see that?

—Beth Harper's a psycho.

—Patty lost it!

In the auxiliary gym, Patty and Beth sat on opposite ends of a long metal bench, separated by a folding table and two stone-faced school resource officers. Ice packs dripped condensation onto the floor.

The door banged open. Two uniformed police officers stepped in—one of them scanned the room with the bored efficiency of someone who'd seen worse on a Tuesday.

"Alright," he said, pulling out a notepad. "We've got assault reports from multiple witnesses, video evidence, the works.

He turned to Beth first.

"Ms. Harper, Ms. Patrick was the aggressor here, based on preliminary witness accounts. She struck first, and you've clearly got visible injuries. Do you want to press charges?"

Beth lowered the ice pack slowly. Her eyes flicked to Patty, who was suddenly very still, staring straight ahead. A slow, deliberate smile tugged at the corner of Beth's mouth, the same one she'd worn when she'd whispered, *'he fucked me stupid.'* She could end this right here—say no, take the slap on the wrist, walk away with the upper hand. Or...

She saw the opening. The chance to twist the knife deeper, to make Patty's victory taste like ash, to drag this out, and she had no other plans for summer.

Beth met the officer's gaze, calm as lake water.

"Yes," she said. "I do. She attacked me unprovoked. I was just defending myself."

Patty's head snapped around so fast the ice pack slipped from her fingers. "You're lying. You—"

"Easy," the second officer cut in, stepping between them. "We'll take statements separately."

Beth leaned back against the cinder-block wall, crossing her arms. "I want to press charges. Full report. Battery, maybe assault with intent—look at my face. She came at me like an animal."

Patty's laugh was short, incredulous, edged with something close to tears. "You're unbelievable. You sleep with my boyfriend, ruin my prom, ruin my graduation, and now you're playing victim?"

Beth shrugged one shoulder, the motion almost elegant despite the blood drying on her chin. "Facts are facts. You hit me. Hard. I've got witnesses. Video. And now I've got the law on my side too."

One of the officers jotted something down on their notepad, waited a moment, and then said, "We'll need to photograph injuries, take formal statements. This could go to the DA. You both understand that?"

Beth nodded, serene. "I understand perfectly."

Patty stared at her across the table, chest heaving. The room felt smaller, the air thicker. For the first time, Patty saw it clearly: Beth didn't just want to win, she wanted to burn everything down and dance in the ashes.

The officers separated them—Patty to one side room, Beth to another. As Beth was led away, she glanced back over her shoulder, catching Patty's eye one last time.

She mouthed two silent words.

Worth it.

Chapter 41

Jailhouse Daughter

Patty sat on the hard plastic chair in the small police station, the fluorescent lights buzzing overhead like angry insects. The air smelled of burnt coffee and disinfectant, with a hint of sweat and fear. Her wrists still ached from where the cuffs had been.

Patty's parents arrived in a rush—her father, Richard, still in his suit from work, tie loosened;

her mother, Karen, in yoga pants and a cashmere wrap, hair pulled back in a hasty ponytail. Their faces were pale, fury and fear warring across their features. Richard spoke to the desk sergeant in low, clipped tones; Karen hovered near Patty, one hand on her hip, one hand on her mouth, like she wanted to chew her out, but not here.

The officer explained the process: citation issued, court date pending, no arrest tonight, no serious injuries. Patty's parents wanted out quickly, no questions asked, beyond the paperwork. The cuffs came off. Patty rubbed her wrists, the red marks throbbing.

Karen's voice was tight. "Let's go..." she sighed.

They walked out into the cool night air. The parking lot was nearly empty—only a few patrol cars and the glow of the station sign. Richard unlocked the Mercedes with a chirp; Patty climbed into the back seat with noticeable shame.

⚕

The car glided down the empty highway, headlights cutting clean tunnels through the dark. Patty hunched down in the backseat like she was trying to disappear. Her knees pressed together tight, her folded hands in her lap latched together so hard that her fingers gripped each other with a painful shakiness. Her eyes scanned slow and heavy, like she was an obvious sinner looking for forgiveness in church. The leather was cold against her thighs. The air conditioning hummed loudly and blew so hard it dried out her eyes.

"Thanks for coming to get me, and bringing me clothes."

They didn't respond for a while.

Karen broke the silence first, voice low and measured.

"You know better, Patricia."

Patty flinched at her full name. It was the same tone her mother used when she'd been caught sneaking vodka from the liquor cabinet in tenth grade.

"You're eighteen," Karen continued. "You're supposed to be an adult. Adults don't get arrested at their own graduation."

Richard's knuckles whitened on the wheel. "Do you have any idea what this could do to your future?" he berated her.

Patty stared at her reflection in the window—smudged mascara, red-rimmed eyes, hair falling out of its bun. She looked small. Pathetic.

"She deserved it," she said quietly.

Karen turned in her seat. "What did you say?" she said with a hint of fury.

Patty's throat closed. "I was angry."

"Anger isn't an excuse," Richard said. "You could lose scholarships. College admissions boards can see your arrests. This isn't a slap on the wrist anymore. You're not a child."

Patty felt the tears come—hot, sudden. She hated them. Hated how weak they made her look.

"I'm sorry," she whispered.

Karen's voice softened—just a fraction. "We're here because we love you. But we're disappointed, Patty. Deeply disappointed."

Richard glanced at her in the rearview mirror. "You've worked so hard. Four years of perfect grades and social accomplishments. And now this? One stupid mishap, and it could all be gone."

Patty pressed her palms to her eyes. "It's not fair."

Karen sighed. "Life isn't fair. You know that."

Patty dropped her hands. Tears streaked her cheeks. "She ruined everything."

Richard's grip tightened on the wheel. "You're going to blame that girl? What's her name... Beth?"

Karen turned fully now. "The police said she's a transfer? From Northwood?"

Patty nodded—fast, desperate. "She's not who she says she is. She's... she's dangerous. She got expelled from there last year. Her ex, Johnny, said she killed his brother."

"Killed?" her mother questioned with a concerned crackle. "Patty..."

Richard slowed the car. "This is... a lot." He rubbed his temple, "Don't you go digging, Patty. Stay out of it. Please."

Chapter 42
Buried in Dirt

P atty was still so furious late into the next day, eyes glowing with a red heaviness from the many hours she sat awake crying last night. Graduation had been a blur—she was certain there was much to, it caps tossed, diplomas clutched, the whole senior class at house parties that lasted until dawn. But she missed it all, thanks to Beth, while everyone else was celebrating freedom, Patty was fuming, sitting in a cell.

Patty slammed her phone down on the kitchen table so hard that the screen cracked a little. "That bitch," she muttered, pacing the marble floor of her parents' empty kitchen. The house was silent—Mom at yoga, Dad at the office—leaving her alone with the rage boiling in her chest.

Her parents were right; Beth could ruin her life forever. With a criminal record, her chances of getting accepted into any university would absolutely tank. The tables had flipped faster than Patty had ever imagined.

"No." Patty stopped pacing, grabbed her laptop from the counter, and dropped into a stool. She wasn't letting Beth win. She wasn't Prom Queen for no reason. If Beth had skeletons—and the Northwood rumors said she did—Patty was going to drag them out, into the light, piece by piece.

She started simple: social media, but nothing there. Given the fact that she was trying to disappear from Northwood, that was no surprise. She'd have to dig deeper. She searched 'Beth Harper' in the local news archives, but still, nothing.

Next: yearbooks. She found the Northwood yearbooks online. She scrolled fast—Club photos, sports, the cheer spread, none featuring Beth. She flipped through the Junior section to H. There she was, Beth Harper, in her typical look and fashion. But in the memorial section at the back—usually for pets or grandparents—there was a full-page dedication.

<u>In loving memory of Tyler Reed. Gone too soon. Forever in our hearts.</u>

Tyler Reed. Johnny's last name was Reed. Patty's pulse kicked up. The page had photos: Tyler in a Northwood football jersey, number 33, grinning with an arm around Johnny. Another of him at prom. A candid in the hallway, laughing with friends. The obituary-style blurb below: *'Tyler was killed in a tragic car accident on April 15th. He was 18. He will be missed by his family, his team, and all who knew his kind spirit.'*

Patty opened a new tab, fingers flying. 'Northwood High School student death car accident, April.'

Local news sites popped up—small-town papers with archives still online.

She skimmed over the headline, 'Northwood Teen Killed— Car Crash—Alcohol—Tree.'

The article was short, dated April 16th last year:

> Tyler Reed, 18, a senior at Northwood High School, was killed late Friday night when his vehicle veered off road and struck a tree... Police say they have an anonymous tip about a minor teen girl who may have been at the scene with the driver, but as of this time, she's not considered a suspect...

Patty leaned back, mouth gaping. That was big. Expulsion made sense now—but why? She dug deeper. Bingo.

Another article dated June 2nd: 'Criminal Charges Dropped in Northwood Crash.'

Prosecutors announced today that vehicular manslaughter charges against the 17-year-old, who an anonymous source's tip says was the true driver in the April crash that killed Tyler Reed, have been dropped due to insufficient evidence. Forensic analysis of the vehicle returned no substantial proof that anyone other than Tyler Reed was driving. The accused attorney argued that over a dozen witnesses placing her at a party was more than enough proof that she was not involved. The district attorney's office agreed, stating, 'We cannot prove beyond a reasonable doubt that the accused [redacted] was ever at the scene.' The teen girl faces expulsion from the school for physical altercations with several students in the past month, as a response to derogatory comments made toward her related to the matter. Reed's family expressed disappointment but declined further comment.

Patty's mind raced. If Beth *was*—and if she knew anything about Beth, she was—there had to be a reason. Why was she driving? Where were they going? Or coming from?

Patty switched to social media archives. She searched Tyler's name—his profile was memorialized, posts frozen in time. Scrolling back to April: tributes from friends, photos of Tyler at games, at parties. One post from Johnny:

'Rest easy, big bro. Love you forever.'

#JusticeForTyler

A hashtag? She clicked it.

Dozens of posts—mostly from Northwood kids. Memes, candles, vigils. Then a thread:

- Everyone knows Beth Harper was driving.

- She was texting Johnny right before the crash.

- Beth Harper killed Tyler. Why isn't she in jail?

- Heard her dad's a lawyer. Bought her way out.

- Expelled but no charges? Bullshit.

Patty's pulse hammered. Texting. That was the key.

Patty leaned back in her stool, laptop screen glowing blue on her face. It all fit. Beth—distracted, texting Johnny while driving his drunk brother home from a party. Why doesn't he have more evidence?

Patty's fingers flew; this was right up her alley. She'd heavily considered a career in crime scene investigation, or something similar at least—and if she was going to walk into a law school with a criminal record, there's no better way to redeem herself than to bring Beth Harper to justice.

Chapter 43

Unanswered Questions

Patty wasn't letting Beth win this. Not after everything—the squad drama, the rumors, the way Beth had slithered into Oakridge like a virus and infected her life right down to the core. If Beth was pressing charges, Patty needed leverage. Real leverage. The Northwood stuff she'd dug up was gold, but incomplete. She needed proof that Beth couldn't deny.

She messaged him on social media.

> We need to talk. About Beth.

The reply came in under five minutes.

> Not here.

> Then where? It's important.

> Diner on 5th. 2pm.

Patty stared at the screen, heart kicking up. Perfect. She'd bring everything.

✝

The diner was a relic—booths of cracked red vinyl, counter stools spinning lazily at the juice bar. The smell of grease and coffee hung thick in the air, striking her nostrils like fire on the hairs. Several neon signs buzzed in the window, looking more out of place than decorative. The jukebox in the corner was playing some old country song about lost love and heartbreak. Patty arrived early—1:50 p.m.—and claimed a booth in the back, away from the lunch crowd of truckers and strange stragglers. She spread her 'Beth Dirt' folder across the table: printed articles, screenshots, yearbook scans, and notes scribbled in red pen. Her laptop sat open, browser tabs ready.

Johnny walked in at 2:02—tall, broad, dark hair messy under a backward cap, wearing a gray hoodie and jeans. He looked tired—bags under his eyes, jaw set like he was chewing on something bitter. He spotted her, nodded once, and slid into the booth seat opposite to her.

"What's this about?" he asked without preamble, voice low and rough.

Patty didn't waste time. She pushed the folder across the table. "Beth. I know about the accident. Tyler. The expulsion. All of it."

Johnny's face went still. He flipped open the folder—eyes scanning the headlines, the memorial page, the dropped charges article. His jaw tightened; a muscle ticked in his cheek.

"And? Tell me something I don't know," he muttered.

"I think I can bring her to justice," she said, "but I need your help."

He closed the folder—slow, controlled—but his hands shook slightly. "What do you need?"

Patty leaned forward, elbows on the table. "Proof. Real proof. You were texting her that night, right? When she was driving Tyler home. Why don't you have evidence? Phone records, screenshots—anything? Something to nail her with."

Johnny looked away—toward the window, the parking lot baking under the afternoon sun. The slow roll of cars glinted the sun into his eyes; a semi-truck rumbled past on the highway, lightly shaking the entire establishment.

"It's not that simple," he said finally.

Patty's eyes narrowed. "Why not? You're his brother. You want justice, don't you?"

Johnny exhaled hard through his nose. He pulled out his phone and opened the messages app. He scrolled back—way back—to last April.

"Here," he said, sliding the phone across. "I saved everything, but it's not what you think."

Patty took the phone, heart racing. The thread was labeled "Beth ♥"—old heart emoji still there, a ghost from before. She scrolled to April 15th.

8:47 p.m.

The party is lit. Where are you?

8:50 p.m.

The game is just wrapping up. We won.

Be there after I get home and shower.

9:12 p.m.

Tyler is trashed.

He wants to go home.

9:13 p.m.

Should I pick you guys up?

9:15 p.m.

He's trying to leave.

I'm gonna try to stop him.

Patty scrolled back through the messages a few more times, face in awe.

"What? If she was walking home, why didn't she see his truck?"

Johnny shook his head. "She wasn't walking home, she was driving."

Patty's brow furrowed. "But why didn't they question her about seeing the truck?"

Johnny leaned back, arms crossed. "Fair point, but the DA said the timeline was too vague—could've been stopped at a light or something. No forensic link. And if her DNA was there, it could've been from going with him, not leaving with him. That's the official story."

Patty stared at the screen, mind turning. Something didn't fit. The articles' said Tyler was found in the driver's seat—alone. If Beth was driving, how did Tyler end up there? And where did Beth go? Uninjured? She just... walked away?

⚕

She scrolled the messages again—slower this time. She looked at her notes. The crash was reported at 9:35 p.m., according to the news article. Patty knew County Road 12 was rather rural, and it was at least a ten-minute drive to any neighborhood outside of Wood Ridge city limits. Enough time for a crash, but...

Patty pondered the facts for several minutes. 'Single occupant—pronounced dead at the scene.'

She looked up at Johnny. "If Beth was driving, why was Tyler alone? In the driver's seat?"

Johnny's face went pale. "What?"

Patty's pulse hammered. Pieces clicking. "She covered it up."

Johnny looked up—sharp, confused. "Patty, I already know all this. Can I go now?"

"Think. She's driving. Texting you. Distracted. She's unhurt—driver's side less damaged. Panics. Drags Tyler's body to the driver's seat, makes it look like he was driving alone. Wipes her prints or whatever and walks away. No one even knows she was there."

Johnny's hands shook. "Yes, Patty, this is what I've been trying to tell you. It's hopeless. I want revenge more than anyone, but please, stop reminding me."

Patty pulled up another tab—she searched for comparisons of autopsy inconsistencies in car crashes. "Passenger injuries: often dashboard knee impacts, whiplash from the side. Driver: steering wheel chest trauma, airbag burns if deployed. If Tyler had passenger wounds but was in the driver's seat... maybe they missed it. Small town coroner. Ruled accident fast."

She scrolled through the coroner report: *'...knee fractures—no airbag residue—wrists unbroken.'*

Patty's eyes gleamed. "That's our proof, if we can get it, she staged the scene. Vehicular manslaughter plus tampering with evidence. Obstruction. We just have to connect the dots."

Johnny's jaw set. "How do you suppose we do that?"

Chapter 44

I've Got the Proof

P atty's eyes darted between her laptop screen and Johnny's phone, the pieces slotting together like a puzzle she hadn't realized was incomplete until now. The coroner's report—county archives—outdated sites. The evidence was sparse, but the details screamed inconsistency if you knew what to look for. She'd cross-referenced it with forensic articles on crash victim positioning, the kind of stuff true-crime podcasts obsessed over, but the small-town DAs might have glossed past it in a rush to close the case.

"Look at this," Patty said, spinning her laptop toward Johnny. The screen showed the autopsy summary: **Cause of death:** *Blunt force trauma to head and chest from vehicular impact. BAC: 0 .18%. Injuries include bilateral patellar fractures (knees), abrasions to left clavicle extending diagonally to right iliac crest (consistent with restraint device), no chemical residue from sodium azide or similar on skin/clothing, no sternal contusion or rib fractures typical of steering column impact, wrists intact with no defensive fractures.*

Johnny frowned, leaning in. "English, please. I read this a year ago—it just says he crashed drunk."

"That's the point," Patty whispered urgently, her voice low in the diner booth. "They assumed he was driving because he was found in the driver's seat. But these injuries? They're textbook passenger side. First, the seatbelt mark: in a standard U .S. car, the driver's seatbelt crosses from the right shoulder down to the left hip. That leaves a bruise starting on the right clavicle. Passenger? It's the opposite—left shoulder to right hip. Tyler's abrasion is left to right. He was buckled in as the passenger."

Johnny's eyes widened, but he shook his head. "Could be a fluke. Seatbelts twist around and stuff."

"Not likely," Patty countered, pulling up a tab from a forensic pathology site she'd bookmarked. "Experts use this to ID positions in crashes all the time—it's admissible in court. And the knees: bilateral fractures from slamming into the dashboard. Passengers get that because their legs are straight out, no pedals or footwell bracing like the driver has. Drivers usually have ankle or tibia breaks from stomping the brake, not knees. Tyler has zero pedal-related injuries, like an abrasion on the right inner ankle from the brake edge, that are common for drivers reacting to a crash."

She scrolled to another section of the report: **Airbag deployment**: *'Driver's side airbag fully deployed per vehicle inspection. No passenger*

airbag deployment noted (possible sensor malfunc-tion or unoccupied).' "See? The driver's airbag went off—that sprays residue like talc or sodium azide all over the driver's face, chest, and arms. Tyler had none. Zero. If he was driving, he'd be covered in it. But as a passenger? His side never deployed. Maybe he was lying down or sitting in the middle. No residue means he wasn't registered as sitting in that seat when it happened."

Johnny rubbed his temples, the weight sinking in. "The cops said the passenger airbag was faulty. It's an older vehicle; they didn't even think twice."

"Exactly—overlooked because it fit their narrative: solo driver, drunk, veers off. But there's more." Patty flipped to the forensic addendum, a short paragraph tacked on from the crime scene techs. **Latent prints:** *'Vehicle interior dusted. Driver's side door handle: no prints matching decedent. Passenger side grab handle and door interior: some prints matching decedent. Steering wheel, gear shift, and ignition area: no recoverable prints—surfaces appear smudged, possibly from environmental exposure.'*

"No prints on the wheel," Patty said, her voice rising with excitement before she caught herself, halfway standing in excitement. She plopped back down, whispering, "Think about it. Tyler's prints are everywhere on the passenger side—like he was bracing there during the crash, grabbing the handle as the car swerved. But the steering wheel? Clean. Not even *his* prints. If he was driving, his hands would've been all over it—sweat, oils, everything. No prints means someone wiped it down after the fact. If you ask me, Beth staged the scene, she probably crashed while distracted texting you, panicked, checks Tyler—no pulse. She's unhurt because the tree hit his side. Then she dragged his body across the bench to the driver's seat and wipes the wheel and shift to erase her touch. She surely forgot to wipe the rest of the car or didn't have time. Walks away, texts you later to cover it up."

Patty scrolled on her laptop a bit more. "Do you have a picture of his truck from the crash?"

Johnny pulled out his phone again, "This one, from the official police report."

"See, right side," Patty said, a reluctant grin forming.

Johnny stared at the screen, his face draining of color. The messages on his phone aligned perfectly: her at 9:15 saying she'd try to stop Tyler from leaving drunk, then silence until 10:11. Crash reported at 9:35—plenty of time for the staging and a hasty hike down the rural road to a side street, avoiding the scene as sirens approached.

Johnny nodded slowly, fire replacing the exhaustion in his eyes. "My family has the full scene photos—unredacted, from the lawyer. A trail of blood across the bench, like... like he was dragged. They said it was from the impact throwing him around, but..."

"Overlooked," Patty finished, grinning fiercely. "We take this to a real forensic expert, not some county hack. Get an affidavit. Beth's done." She closed the laptop, the rage from last night transforming into cold resolve. This wasn't just leverage—it was justice, the kind that would bury Beth forever.

Chapter 45
The Setup

The rain hammered on the roof of Beth's small house on the edge of town like fists on a coffin lid. Thunder rolled low and constant, the kind that vibrated in your teeth. Streetlights flickered, half-dead in the downpour. Johnny stood on the porch under the weak yellow bulb, soaked through his hoodie, hair plastered to his forehead. He knocked once—firm, deliberate.

The door opened a crack. Beth's face appeared, pale, eyes wide and wary. She was in an oversized

T-shirt and leggings, hair loose, no makeup. For a second, she looked almost like the girl from last April, before everything broke.

"Johnny?" Her voice cracked. "What are you doing here?"

He lifted his chin, water dripping from the brim of his cap. "I'm done fighting it. I'm ready to forgive you."

She stared at him, searching his face for the lie. Then something in her softened—or cracked. She stepped back and opened the door wider. "Come in, before you drown."

⚕

The inside smelled of vanilla candle and damp laundry. The living room was dim, lit only by a single lamp, and the blue stutter of the television, complimented by the smooth hum of the volume chirping on low. Beth shut the door behind him and locked it. She hugged herself.

"I never wanted any of this," she said quietly, not quite meeting his eyes. "Tyler... he was drunk, he wouldn't listen. I tried to stop him from driving. I swear I tried. I've carried it every single day since. I'm so sorry, Johnny. For everything."

She didn't say she was driving. She didn't say she dragged his brother's body across the seat to cover it up. She didn't say she wiped the wheel clean. Just sorry. The word hung between them like smoke in the eyes.

Johnny said nothing. He let her close the distance.

She reached up, tentative, and slowly brushed the wet hair from his forehead. Then she kissed him—soft at first, testing. When he didn't pull away, she pressed harder, hands sliding under his hoodie, peeling it off. His shirt followed. She guided him backward through the hallway, lips never leaving his, until they reached her bedroom. "You're right, I owe you, big time."

The bed was unmade, sheets tangled. Lightning flashed through the blinds, throwing stark white bars across their bodies. Beth stripped down to black lace underwear, climbed over him, straddling his hips. Her kisses turned quick and desperate. Fingers trailed down his chest, lower, working the button of his jeans. She rested against him, breathing deep and slow, trying to lose herself in the heat, in the lie that this could fix anything.

But something was wrong.

His hands stayed at his sides. No answering grip. No heat in his eyes. Just stillness.

She arched up, hanging over him, searching his face. "Johnny?"

He looked up at her, calm. Too calm.

"I'll be right back," she whispered, sliding down and off him. She disappeared into the hallway.

⚕

Johnny lay there in his boxers, staring at the ceiling, listening to the rain and the thunder and the soft creak of floorboards. For a moment is was all too familiar, like nothing changed between them, like the past year never even happened, like they were back to careless lovers. His mind slipped into somewhere safe. He didn't think of Tyler right away; he'd forgotten why he was there just long enough to let the plan unravel. His phone was silent in the pocket of his discarded jeans. No text to Patty. The plan was already off the rails.

Beth returned barefoot, right hand behind her back.

She climbed onto the bed again, straddling him once more. This time her smile was different—thin, trembling.

"Why," she said softly, "did you have to go digging again?"

The blade came out fast—a sharp, pointed cooking knife, still wet from the dish rack. She drove it down into his chest over and over. Each thrust punctuated by desperate words.

"Why—did—you—have—to—go—digging—again—"

Johnny gasped, blood bubbling at his lips with every desperate breath. His hands came up weakly, not to fight, but to hold her wrists for a second—like he was steadying her.

With his last breath, barely audible over the storm, he said it deep into her soul, "It's all over, love."

His head lolled. Eyes open, staring past her at nothing.

Beth turned in shock when she heard it. Suddenly, the front door exploded inward, followed by quick, echoing yells for Johnny.

Knife still buried to the hilt. Blood pooled dark on the sheets. Beth froze as she watched Patty stumble through the threshold of her room, rain-soaked, wild-eyed, almost breathless.

She'd waited several minutes past the agreed signal—no text, no check-in.

She saw Johnny first—motionless, chest a ruin of red, then she saw Beth—knife in hand, staring at her.

Patty screamed once, short and raw. Quick to draw her phone, but her hands trembled as her thumb fumbling around as she dialed 9-1-1, bringing it to her ear with an uncontrolled shake and shiver.

"9-1-1, what's your—"

Before she could answer, she found Beth's blood-slick hand clamped over her mouth, the knife at her throat. "Drop it. Drop it now."

Patty's phone clattered to the floor. The call stayed connected—muffled voices asking for location.

Beth dragged her backward toward the hallway. "Move."

She pulled Johnny's car keys from his pants on the ground. Beth snatched them, shoved Patty ahead of her through the ruined front door, and into the storm. She forced her into the passenger seat of Johnny's Jeep, slammed the door, and ran around to the driver's side.

The engine roared up with a grumble. Tires spun on wet gravel, then caught. The Jeep fishtailed out, quickly covering ground out of the neighborhood, and jumped out onto County Road 12—empty and black, rain sheeting across the windshield.

Beth drove erratically, swerving between lanes, headlights barely cutting through the downpour. Her hands shook on the wheel; blood streaked the leather.

Patty pressed herself against the door, breathing hard. "We have the proof, Beth. You killed

Tyler. Vehicular manslaughter, evidence tampering—hell, leaving the scene. And now… murder? You're going away for a long time."

"Shut up!" Beth screamed, voice cracking. "Shut up, shut up, shut up!"

"Listen to me. Police are already on their way. They have the call. They'll trace the Jeep. Give yourself up, Beth, it's over."

Beth's foot pressed harder on the gas. The speedometer climbed—60, 70, 80. The road blurred. Lightning cracked overhead, illuminating her face in stark flashes: tears, mascara, blood.

Patty kept her voice steady despite the knife still trembling in Beth's hand while she drove.

"It's over, Beth, listen…"

The sound of sirens started to carry in—distant at first, then closer.

Chapter 46

It's All Over, Love

The police radio crackled through the storm like static lightning.

The perusing vehicle came over the radio, "Dispatch, Unit 7 on scene. Anticipated female hostage confirmed."

A second voice, calmer, colder, "Dispatch, this is Unit 11, we're at the scene of the original call, one male victim confirmed deceased, looks to be stab wounds. Send us CSI. Scene secured.

Then the dispatch relayed, "Responding officers be advised; suspect may be armed with a knife, believed to be highly agitated."

The sergeant's voice cut in, low and steady, "All units, be careful on entry. Primary objective: secure the hostage. Do not engage unless the suspect presents an immediate lethal threat. Repeat: secure the hostage."

The rain lashed the windshield of the lead cruiser as tires hissed across wet asphalt. Red and blue lights painted the night in frantic strokes.

Inside the stolen Jeep, Beth's knuckles gripped over the wheel hopelessly, running red and blue like the lights. Rain sheeted down the glass in relentless curtains. She glanced in the rearview mirror again—red and blue pulsing behind them now, growing brighter, larger, louder, closer with every heartbeat. The sirens wailed, a rising scream that swallowed the thunder.

Her foot slammed the gas pedal harder. The engine roared. The speedometer needle swung past 90, past 100, trembling toward 110. The Jeep fishtailed on the slick road, tires losing purchase, then clawing it back.

Patty pressed herself against the passenger door, seatbelt cutting into her chest. "Beth, please—slow down! You're going to kill us both. It's wet out here!"

Beth didn't answer. Her breathing was ragged, eyes wild in the dashboard glow. Tears mixed with rain on her cheeks. "They're not taking me," she muttered. "This is all *your* fault!"

The Jeep hydroplaned. Beth overcorrected—too hard, too fast. The rear end swung out. Tires screeched. The world tilted.

The tree loomed out of the darkness—massive, scarred, bark blackened from old impact. The same tree.

The Jeep struck it dead-center. Metal screamed. Glass exploded. The airbag punched Patty in the face like a brick made of fists. The world went white, then black.

When Beth came to, her head throbbed. Blood trickled from a gash above her left eyebrow. The Jeep was crumpled around her, hood folded like paper, steam hissing from the engine. The windshield was spiderwebbed, rain pouring through the shattered driver's-side window.

She looked over. Patty was slumped against the door, unconscious, airbag deflated across her lap, a thin line of blood running from her nose. Her chest rose and fell—alive, but out cold.

Beth's hands shook as she unbuckled. She reached for the knife—still sticky with Johnny's blood. Then she leaned over, cut her loose, and then grabbed Patty under the arms and dragged her limp body across the console.

Beth swung open the driver's side door with a groan. Cold rain poured over them as she stepped out. She hauled Patty out into the mud and gravel, letting her plop—almost lifelessly—against the ground.

Headlights swept the scene. Sirens crescendoed. Three cruisers skidded to a stop twenty yards away, with doors flying open. Officers poured out, weapons drawn, flashlights cutting through the downpour.

"Police! Show us your hands!"

Beth yanked Patty upright, one arm locked around her chest, the knife pressed to the soft skin under her jaw. Patty's eyes snapped open, dazed, terrified.

"Stay back!" Beth screamed. A thunderous storm of emotion on her face. Her voice cracked, "Stay the fuck back, or I'll cut her!"

Patty gasped, hands coming up instinctively. "Beth—please—"

"Tell them it's okay, Patty! Tell them it's okay!" Beth's voice cracked, shrill, frantic. "Tell them I didn't do it! Tell them it was an accident—tell them! Tel"

The officers fanned out, slow and deliberate, rain streaming off their raincoats. Flashlights pinned Beth and Patty in harsh white beams.

"Drop the knife!" the lead officer shouted. "Drop it now and put your hands up! Nobody needs to get hurt!"

Beth's arm tightened around Patty's ribs. The blade trembled against her throat. "I said, stay back!"

Patty's scream tore out of her—blood-curdling, primal. It echoed off the trees, cut through the rain like a blade. "Help me!"

Two officers held the ground while more officers arrived on scene.

Eventually—for Patty, it felt like a lifetime, for Beth, it felt almost instantaneous—more officers arrived on scene. Surrounding them with squad cars that poured out more officers with more guns, pointing right at them.

An officer crept around the back of the circle of cars and carefully moved in under the cover of the heavy rain and glimmering darkness, and quickly tackled Beth from behind, driving her down into the mud. The knife clattered away. Another officer yanked Patty free, pulling her back behind the line of cruisers.

Beth thrashed, screaming incoherently—words lost in sobs and thunder. "No—no—no—you can't—she made me—she made me—"

They forced her face down into the mud, knees in her back. Cold metal cuffs snapped around her wrists. Tears and rain puddled around her face.

Patty was quickly wrapped in a blanket as paramedics swarmed her. She stared at the wrecked Jeep, at the tree that had ended Tyler Reed's life exactly one year and three months earlier. The irony hung thick in the air, heavier than the storm.

Beth was dragged to her feet, hair plastered to her face, mascara running in black rivers. She looked at Patty one last time—eyes wide, pleading, broken.

Patty looked back. No pity. No mercy. Just cold, exhausted certainty.

Still in her underwear—shivering in the cold, wet, and stormy night—the officers led Beth to the back of a cruiser and sat her inside. Beth wiped the mud and mascara from her face with her arm, sweeping a few painful inhales through her as her eyes swelled.

A single tear ran down her face as the door slammed shut.